MERRY
HANUKKAH

DEBBY CARUSO

Merry Hanukkah

Copyright © 2018 Debby Caruso

ISBN-13: 978-1-7325190-0-8

Book cover design and interior formatting by Tugboat Design

For Scott, Enzo, and Dagny
My very own
Holy Trinity

Chapter One

It's more perfect than I imagined. I look around, but I feel as if I'm standing outside myself as I breathe in the garden.

I look to James and see him framed by gorgeous flowers and all forms of greenery, things I can't even hope to pronounce, and I smile.

Our eyes hold for a long moment, and then I let loose a conspiratory giggle.

"I DO!" I practically shout. I turn to acknowledge the crowd as I hear loud clapping and a wolf whistle, and I'm sure I'm grinning from ear to ear. And as I turn back to both the Priest and the Rabbi standing behind us, halfway under the chuppa, we kiss that first sweet kiss.

Out of the corner of my eye I see the Priest and the Rabbi bump into each other, eagerly waiting to give the next instruction, however I am consumed with James, passionately kissing, standing in the center of my long-held dream.

When we part, I catch Uncle Ben's eye. Apparently my grin is contagious.

"James, we still have a glass here that looks like it needs breaking," the Rabbi instructs.

We share a look. James snatches the linen-wrapped glass out of the hand of the hovering rabbi, and at the moment that his foot crushes the glass, the right side of the assembled guests shouts out, "Mazel Tov!"

And the left side, "Amen!"

Chapter Two

I've decided I never want to stop dancing. I look up and see the white lights strung from every corner, held together in a gorgeous arrangement right above my head in the center of the tent. There's a crowd around us now, and as James pulls me close, I hear several "oohs" and "aahs" hit the air. He pulls me in, grabs a quick kiss, and then extends his arm so I dance away in a flirtatious maneuver we had practiced once or twice.

There is a seven piece band on the stage playing "L-O-V-E," and as the song ends, the lead singer of the band calls everyone's attention.

"Oh! Rhonda and James...you two are too...are too..." She doesn't finish the sentence, rather begins making strange hand gestures and blinking wildly at the crowd. Then she laughs maniacally, as if she is in on some sort of hilarious joke. She is the stereotype of a wedding singer gone bad: a late-fifties wanna-be rock star with high hair, heavy lipstick, and exaggerated enthusiasm. She stops abruptly, then carries on. "Well! Well! We've got a special request from Uncle...Ben!"

I hear her mumbling then, half-into the microphone, as she grabs a piece of wadded-up paper and adjusts her skirt, "Oh, like the rice!"

I cannot imagine what she's been drinking all night, and decide it's no big deal as long as she stays standing. And singing.

Uncle Ben crosses the dance floor and steals me away from James. At that moment, the band lurches into a raucous rendition of "Help Me Rhonda" by the Beach Boys.

He starts it.

We begin shouting the lyrics back and forth, all while dancing and laughing. We're making a spectacle of ourselves and we don't care one whit, and as I come up for air, I see James with a great big smile, drinking us in from the sideline.

Uncle Ben pulls me close and whispers in my ear.

"You, my dear, are more than I ever hoped for James." Then he twirls me.

As I come back, I almost shout. "Uncle Ben, you're the best!"

He winks, and we finish the song with flair. As we exit the dance floor, I nod towards my mother-in-law, who is chain-smoking and scowling at me from a nearby table.

"I only wish she felt the same."

"Viv? Please, don't let my sister-in-law bother you. She's only happy when she's miserable." He laughs a loud and hearty laugh, and gives me a pat on the shoulder. "Now go find your husband."

I cross the dance floor to find James in conversation with his grandfather.

I put my arm around his waist, and my head on his shoulder. I take a moment to listen to the banter between them.

"I agree, Grandpa. I'm going to have Uncle Ben light the first cigar later on, and Grandma shouldn't say anything because tonight is a special night."

I try to hide my grin in James's sleeve.

"Rhonda, take notes, dear. A man needs a cigar on a night such as this." He nods his head sagely, but there is a twinkle in his eye.

I reach down to plant a big kiss on his cheek. He turns his wheelchair more towards me.

"Grandpa, I not only agree, I may just join in the festivities right along with you fellas."

"Really?" Grandpa gives James a worried look.

"She's joking, Grandpa." James turns to face me. "Grandpa isn't that progressive." He pulls a face and I stifle a giggle. After a few more moments, we decide to eat something…finally. People warned me that you never get a chance to eat on your wedding day, but I never did take them seriously.

"I'm famished!" I say this to James through a huge hunk of bread that I just stuffed in my mouth sideways. I'm about to wash it down with some wine when Desiree comes barreling up to me.

"Conference! Ladies Lounge! Presto! Change-o! Now!"

I am chewing and making hand gestures towards my plate, to no avail. I should know better. Desiree is a force that will not be denied.

"You've got your whole lives to eat together. Come! Now!" Desiree begins to tug on my arm. She smiles benignly at James. "This will only take a sec."

James, his mouth crammed with food, nods and makes some sort of hand gesture as if to say, "Go."

The next thing I know I am being pulled across the dance floor by my maid of honor. In the shuffle, I grab another drink off the tray of a passing waiter.

"Thanks!" I call to him.

"And Dez! This dress only goes about FIVE MPH! I'm coming! Chill out!" I'm trying to drink and not spill in a two thousand pound frock of white.

"I don't want you to miss this."

We make a circuitous route through the reception and into the house, navigating a narrow corridor, and then pulling to a stop outside an ornate door with a flower painted on it.

Desiree presses her finger to her lips and then ushers me inside the door. We stand silently in the anteroom and after a moment begin to hear voices from the room adjacent. Desiree puts her head up against the adjoining wall and motions me closer. We're trying to eavesdrop over the sound of toilets flushing and running water at the sink.

"All I'm saying, Viv, is that you better get it together. You're a little happy already, and we still have to take family pictures. Plus, look at your lipstick!" Aunt Bunny makes a tsk-tsk sound that echoes in the bathroom, and Dez and I are just about holding it together ourselves.

"I don't care about my lipstick! And I am decidedly *not* happy! How would you feel if someone you barely knew came along and kidnapped your son?!"

Desiree looks at me and makes a crazy signal while mouthing the word, "*Kidnapped?*"

I almost throw up in my mouth, but flash Dez a huge eye roll instead.

"Oh, for gosh sakes, Viv! Spare me the melodrama! I need more hairspray." This from Aunt Bunny.

"You don't understand. I need another drink." And then Vivian hiccups.

We hear shuffling sounds then, so at that very moment, Dez lunges for the door, slams it, and begins chattering loudly, as if in mid-conversation.

"Well, hello ladies!" Aunt Bunny exclaims. I stare at a woman who does not need another ounce of hairspray. Ever.

"Well, hello to you!" Desiree smiles broadly. "Just helping Rhonda take a pee...you know how it is, a thousand pounds of dress and all..."

Vivian looks me up and down as if sizing up the competition and quickly exits the lounge on unsteady legs.

"What exactly was that?" I stare after them in wonder, not sure what we just walked in on, but determined not to care.

"Who knows?" Dez shakes her head. "Now let me help you with that dress."

Chapter Three

After tidying up my desk and putting everything in its proper place, I decided to take a look at my calendar, just to get an idea of the final few months of the year.

As I shuffle through, my thoughts turn to the holiday season. I wonder what falls when, and as I make my way to the last month of the year, my eyes zero in on the following:

December 25: Christmas Day
December 26: Hanukkah Begins

I can barely contain myself as I jump up from my desk and begin pacing, my time honored tradition for all things deep thought. After a moment, I lunge across my newly straightened desk and stab the intercom.

"Desiree Logan, please report to me!"

"Yes, Ma'am!" She shouts back at me.

By the time Dez enters I'm about to burst.

I smile at my dear friend and partner in crime, then try to contain myself as I settle back into my chair.

I wait patiently as Dez folds herself into the chair facing me.

"What's up? Did the cleaning people mess up your bookshelves again?" She leads with a mischievous grin.

I shoo away her thought, and then turn the calendar to face her. I point to the two dates, my freshly manicured nail underlining them as punctuation.

"Dez, tell me! Could I have planned this any better?!"

"Planned? What?"

"Look!" I'm about to jump across the desk.

Desiree looks again and notices the near convergence of the two holidays.

"Oh God, Rhon...you could make a week-long festival at your place...!" She teases me, then turns the calendar back in my direction.

"Don't make fun! This is a great opportunity for me! I can merge our traditions and maybe even impress Vivian..." My mind is whirring.

"Of course! Because that's what the holidays are all about... impressing Vivian!"

"Well, not just that! I mean..." I persist.

"Rhonda, think about it! What's the *real* reason for the holidays anyway?"

"It's about having the Perfect Day! Or Days...in this case." I'm musing now.

"I thinketh not. I vaguely remember something about Holy Days...but either way..." She gestures as if this thought is ultimately unimportant. "It's about sharing a special day with the various players in the game that populate your life throughout the year, except you give out gifts, and get drunk, and pretend you really like each other."

"Dez! This from the woman who hides every year at the local shelter and can't be called upon to help with anything remotely holiday!" She forgets that I know her really, really well.

"Surely you jest. What about the year you had pneumonia *and* the flu? Who wrapped all your thousands of presents?"

"Fine, you win. You wrapped." I'll give her that.

"You even convinced me to wrap the Toys for Tots presents, which I knew had to be given unwrapped!"

"I still don't get that." I shake my head.

"It doesn't matter." She's almost glaring at me. "The Marines run the thing. You should listen to the Marines!"

"Okay! Dez! We are veering off course here! If I am going to do this, I'm going to need your help! I may need you to pitch in around the house, and elf a little with me."

"My Christmas plans are iron-clad, kid. I can't let the shelter down."

"I'm talking Hanukkah here!"

Dez pauses. "Does Hanukkah have elves?"

"Does it matter? I need your help in order to make this the perfect day for James and his family!"

"Have you even talked to James about this? I mean, is he on board with the whole Hanukkah thing?"

I shrug.

"What is there not to like? I intend to have the perfect day, with perfect food, perfect desserts, perfect presents...! I mean, I'm willing to do what it takes to make this Hanukkah the best one James has ever had...not to mention Vivian, and Vlad...oh, and Uncle Ben and Aunt Bunny!"

"Grandma and Grandpa..." Dez adds.

"Cousins Jill and Ira..." I am making a mental list now.

"Ugh, do you have to invite Jill?"

"Yes, Jill has to be invited." Now it's my turn to glare. "I know you don't care for her, but Dez, she's family now. You have to be nice...for me." And I attempt to bat my eyelashes.

"I'll be nice until the time comes to not be nice anymore," she sneers.

"What's that supposed to mean?"

"It means...have a fork handy so that I can plunge it into her eye if necessary."

"Hey! Dez! I need you to start thinking Holy Day thoughts here!"

"Rhonda, I have to go." Dez gets up to exit the office and shoots me a wry grin. "It's July. I am so not ready for *any* holiday yet. I haven't even figured out where I'm hiding for Labor Day."

I roll my eyes and wave her away. "That's okay, you just have to be ready when I need you. And I know you will be the best Hanukkah elf...ever!"

"Not to mention the *first* Hanukkah elf ever..."

"I'll see you in the meeting."

"Later."

Chapter Four

As I walk into the conference room, I see a long line of young people all wearing various shades of black. And I chuckle. We are the epitome of a New York City ad agency. I snag a seat right next to Dez and frown when I notice her coffee. I should have thought to bring one.

"Hey," I tap her coffee cup, "did you grab one for me?"

"Between you and Artie...I needed this just to keep up."

"Ha." As we wait for Artie, I take a general sweep of the surroundings, my eyes combing over the various posters that line the walls. I prefer the flat screens that are looping our commercials on mute, as it makes us seem *très* cutting-edge.

I'm just about to go get a coffee when Artie bounds into the room, full of energy and swagger. He situates himself at the head of the table and nods his head at each individual before proceeding.

"Greetings, Team!"

We acknowledge Artie and I begin to fidget. I need caffeine, regardless of Dez's opinion.

"I've got you all assembled here for the next chapter of SPLASH. I just got off the phone with the CEO of Splash Beverages, and although he loves the last campaign, he has made it clear that he wants a new tag line heading into next year."

A couple of groans; Dez begins tapping her pen. Artie holds his hands up in surrender.

"I know, I know how hard you all worked on the last one. I actually wish we could keep rolling over the whole *"SPLASH INTO IT!"* thing, but the company's going green---hell, the whole world is going green, so our next tag line has to have something green in it, something green about it, right up front."

"So people spend their green." Ramon is a cynic.

"Don't kid yourself, Ramon. I know a whole lot of people who won't spend their money on a company that doesn't do the right thing environmentally," Lola counters.

"You know a whole lot of tree-huggers," Ramon claps back.

This causes an eruption from the group, each person talking over the other about the advantages of going green.

"EITHER WAY! Hey! Look eyes!" Artie does this weird thing with his fingers pointing towards the table and then directly towards his eyes. He doesn't stop until everyone is looking directly at him and there's silence in the room.

"Think green, people! We can do this! We've done it before and we'll do it again! Now, off you go to FORM, STORM, NORM, and PERFORM!"

Everyone begins to get up and exit the room, grabbing up their coffee cups and notebooks. Ramon and Lola exchange a nasty look while Artie fist-bumps another member of the team and says, "Rock On." Dez and I begin to walk back towards our offices, and I'm about to grab my long-awaited coffee when suddenly, Artie calls us back.

"One more thing! We need the new tag line by January 3rd! And I would actually like to have it all sewn up by the break! So...have your fun, take your time, but know that the Jolly Holly-Days will be no fun unless we get to 'SPLASH' into the New Year!"

Dez and I exchange a look as we walk out of the room.

"Great, another tag line for Splash." I shake my head yet again and look at Dez with a wry grin on my face.

"Wanna 'storm?'" I extend my hand out in front of me. "Or... form, norm, perform...?"

"I was thinking more like a cappuccino..." Dez says as she pitches her empty cup into a recycling bin.

"I'm with you. I was dying in there."

So we toss our things on our desks and duck into an elevator. After all, a gal can't come up with groundbreaking ideas unless and until she's properly caffeinated.

Chapter Five

"Sunday really has nothing on Saturday." I announce this as we lie opposite one another on the couch, my feet in his face. There is soft piano music playing in the background, and coffee cups and the remnants of brunch lay on a nearby coffee table. The newspapers are strewn about and the television is on mute nearby.

"Would you like some more coffee?" James moves my feet and begins to get up off the couch. Once up, he comes over to my side, grabs a mug off the table, then leans and plants a delicate kiss on my forehead. I love watching him move.

"I would like more James..." I send what I think is a lascivious look and a wink, then take a deep breath and stretch, languishing on the couch. He goes to pick up my mug, then puts it down and turns back. He falls to his knees then, and begins smothering me with deep, slow kisses, working his way down my neck.

"You know what I would like? More Saturdays..."

His kisses move from my neck, lower, and then he scoops me up in his arms.

"Ah! And just where are you taking me...?" I act as if I am scolding, but we both know better.

"Back to bed. This couch is a bit tiny for what I had in mind."

I can't help but giggle as he wags his eyebrows, and we continue kissing as he carries me from the living room into our bedroom. With a ceremonious air, he deposits me on the bed, and then continues to kiss me deeply. In a flash, we're all over each other, tearing at clothes and knocking throw pillows off the bed. We pause a second and both dive under the covers, laughing as we go.

"It is a little arctic in here."

"Should I lower the AC?" James offers.

"Forget it. Forget everything." I pull him close as we huddle under the covers. Suddenly the phone rings, pulling us from the moment.

"Machine," James mumbles.

"What?" I pull away a bit and focus on the ring.

"I said let the machine get it," James insists.

"Okay."

The phone keeps ringing as we resume kissing. The machine clicks on and I hear myself on the outgoing message. Then we hear Vivian's voice, broken up and shaky.

"James, this is your mother. If you're there, please pick up. Your grandfather is..."

I shove James away and lunge for the phone on the nightstand. As I grab the receiver, I give James a "one sec" hand signal.

"Vivian? Are you okay?"

"Yes, is James there please?"

"Sure, oh, of course. Hold on." I hand the phone to James and I'm instantly worried.

"Mom, what's going on?" He is propped up on one elbow now, listening intently into the phone.

"Okay. Okay. Wow. Okay. Yes. Calm, well…try to calm down. I'll be over in a little bit. Okay. Okay."

I stare at James as he heavily hands me the phone. He says nothing as he lifts himself up off the bed. He turns to me a second later and his face is instantly etched in anguish.

"Grandpa's passed."

I breathe reflexively and after a sharp intake of breath, I instinctively cover my mouth with my hand.

"Oh, no, James. Oh, I am so sorry!" My eyes well up and I am frozen on the bed, watching James shrug on his recently discarded clothes.

"Me too. I've got to get over there. Are you coming?" He looks at me.

"Oh!" Sure. I'm not sure what to do here.

"You're family now, babe. I want you to come. I'm just going to go over to my mother's house and see what needs to be attended to…try and comfort her…I know she loved her father something fierce, and this isn't going to be easy for her or Aunt Bunny. I just can't believe it…I mean, he seemed so great at the wedding, very 'up' and…" He's choking back tears.

"Oh, honey. I am so sorry…of course I'm coming with you. Maybe…should we bring something?"

"I think just ourselves for now. God knows there will be enough food to feed a platoon at the Shiva."

Chapter Six

"I'll get it!" I call this out to no one in particular, as I make my way to the door and greet the deliveryman (woman? person?) that I can barely see hiding behind an enormous fruit basket.

Once signed for, I make my way back into the Shiva call, only to be turned around again by yet another delivery person leaning on the doorbell. I go to hold the door open, and at that point, I feel James arching over me to open the door wider.

"Where do you think we should put these?" James asks as we both take in the two tables that are already overflowing with food in the dining area, as well as a separate array of food on the nearby kitchen table.

"I would ask Aunt Bunny but I don't want to bother her." We were holding the Shiva call at Aunt Bunny and Uncle Ben's house, and I was trying to be both as helpful and as unobtrusive as possible.

He sighs.

"I see you weren't kidding about the food." I take a hold of my basket and place it gingerly on the hall table, this one overflowing with various foodstuffs.

"Hey, baby." James puts down the latest basket and then kisses me gently on the side of my face. Then he lets out another big sigh.

I turn to face James head-on. "You okay?"

James offers me a half-hearted grin.

"It just doesn't seem real. I mean, he was at our wedding…he was just there…"

"I'm so glad he made the wedding." I rub his arm.

"Me too."

"So where should I put these?" I gesture towards all the newly arrived foodstuffs.

"Ah, best that you ask Aunt Bunny. I thought I saw her somewhere near the bar."

"Got it. Okay, so what can I do for you?"

"Nothing, really, just being here is enough."

"Now, where else would I be?" I offer him a loving smile, and extend my hand as we re-enter the living room. All around, various people are milling about with paper plates in hand.

I spy James's cousin Ira in a far corner of the room, pontificating to a handful of callers, with a woman sitting beside him, nodding voraciously at every word he utters.

"And that's why we need to be invested in the program," Ira says as he reaches for a drink.

I decide to gently steer James away from them and into another room where Uncle Ben is setting out fresh bottles of wine, and uncorking the red.

"Hey, Uncle Ben, have you seen Aunt Bunny? I wanted to ask her about the baskets."

Uncle Ben nods, "I think she's visiting with her mother." He gestures away from the bar towards Aunt Bunny, sitting next to an older woman on the screened-in porch. I cross the room then, as Uncle Ben pulls James towards him with a conspiratory grin.

As I'm walking away, I hear him say, "Is your cousin Ira still out there entertaining the mourners?"

I decide to linger and eavesdrop.

"I believe so," James says.

"Hah!" Uncle Ben sniffs, sticks his head around the corner to see where in fact Ira is, then turns back to James. "He was always a pompous kid. Your grandfather preferred you."

"Well, Uncle Ben, I don't think that's..."

"It's true. Either way, I got him but good!"

"What did you do?"

"I got his pompous ass some food off the non-kosher table."

The two men share a laugh and then Uncle Ben points skyward.

"Your grandfather would have loved it!"

I'm still lingering; getting to know this family is a painstaking process. Thank God for Uncle Ben, as he is so down-to-earth and real.

I see them share a look, and then Vivian comes between them.

"What are you two chuckling about?" She offers a quick look of disdain to Uncle Ben, and then turns to James and showers him with a megawatt smile.

"Nothing, Mom...it's just Ira." He shakes his head as if to say that says it all.

"My poor sister, if she weren't already dead, she would *die* to see that Ira turned out just like that idiot she married...Oh, and the wife? What's up with the sudden interest in being Jewish?" Vivian tsks.

"Perhaps she's ready to have a child?" Uncle Ben suggests this, deadpan as possible.

"You think?" James does this little cough-in-his-sleeve maneuver.

"And what does that have to do with the price of tea in China?" Vivian counters.

"Some women..." Uncle Ben starts to reply, but is cut off by Vivian, narrowing her eyes and focusing right in on James.

"Does your wife know that your grandfather would want to see you raise your kids Jewish?"

My heart is beating triple time.

"I think Grandpa..." James begins.

"...could care less as long as they're Yankee fans!" Uncle Ben finishes, and I love him all the more.

Vivian cuts her eyes towards Ben and then tries to fake a laugh. "Don't encourage him."

"I think your grandfather would be very happy to see Rhonda convert, James."

"Mom, we don't need to discuss this right now." He is looking right at me now, and just when I think I'm about to be busted, he excuses himself from his mother and Uncle Ben.

I hear Vivian say, under her breath, "It should have been discussed before the wedding."

We're not even a few feet away from them, and just as I'm about to spontaneously combust, I hear Uncle Ben change the topic.

"Viv, you look like a woman who needs a beverage. And I just uncorked a nice red wine." He begins to pour her a glass of wine as she stands there silently fuming, looking after James. Uncle Ben then turns toward Vivian and puts one arm around her as he places her hand around the glass. He lifts up his own glass and says, "L'Chaim."

Chapter Seven

As we pull up to the graveside, I get out on my side of the car, but wait for James as I see him rounding the back. He reaches for my hand, and we begin down a small slope together, towards James' grandfather's grave. Neither one of us says a word, but it feels sacred somehow, as we descend toward a beautiful sunset.

We locate the grave and James pauses. He takes a deep breath and pulls a battered Yankee cap out of his back pocket, placing it gently at the graveside.

"I don't know how orthodox this is, but I know my grandfather would like it." He begins to choke up and I stand a little bit to the side, giving him a moment. When he finally looks at me, I offer him a teary smile.

"I heard so many great stories today at the Shiva call. I only wish I had gotten more time, to know him even better."

"Ah, but then it would have hurt more to lose him."

"Sometimes that's okay."

"I'll tell you a story nobody told today..." He shrugs and puts his hands in his pockets, then removes them and chokes back tears as he looks out onto the horizon.

I wait patiently for him to go on.

"I remember one year when I was really struggling with baseball. I just couldn't hit a thing. I went from being the best kid on the block to a kid who suddenly stood still as a statue every time the ball went by me. I had gotten hit by a pitch and then I think I was afraid to swing. My grandfather noticed and basically said that we had to 'nip it in the bud'."

We share a smile.

"So, the next day right after school, my grandfather came over with a bucket of baseballs. He set us up right in the backyard and he pitched to me for hours. I can still hear him saying, *'Just swing at it! Swing at everything! If you swing enough, eventually something's gonna connect.'*"

"So did you swing?" I ask.

"After a while, I just began swinging. I missed a lot. I got upset. I wanted to quit. I remember at one point telling my grandfather that I just couldn't do it anymore. But he stayed out there, he stayed out there until it was dark and then even way after that. He told me I could, he encouraged me, he yelled at me, and he kept it up until eventually I was swinging, and we didn't stop until my grandmother rounded the corner in her car and yelled at him to call it a night," James reminisced.

"So he taught you something about perseverance that day." I sighed.

James nods his head. "More than that; he taught me something about family. I overheard my grandmother telling my mother the day after that he overslept an important appointment for work the next day. I guess it all worked out, but I remember I felt guilty about keeping him out all night. When I saw him next, I asked him about it, and he told me not to worry. He said, '*Nothing is as important as being with your family.*'"

"That must have made you feel pretty special. How old were you then?"

"About eleven. I just thought he was a great guy. I mean, I knew it even then. You know, he was the only father I knew until Vlad came along...and then I just think it was a little late."

"For Vlad to be Dad?"

James laughs and looks sideways at me.

"Yeah. I remember my first weekend away at college...moving into the dorm...I kept introducing him as 'My Vlad'." He wraps air quotes around the words and chuckles.

"Did anyone notice?"

"If they did, they didn't say anything." James smiles, then looks around him. "I need a rock."

I reach into my pocket and pull out two. I extend my hand towards James.

"I bought two."

"One of the many reasons I love you."

Chapter Eight

It's Monday morning and I have all my favorite Monday morning things assembled in one room: Dez across from me, a hot latte on my right, and some upbeat jazz playing on my office speakers.

I figure it could be worse.

"How about...'*Splash Into Green?*'" Dez suggests.

"I just think it's too much like the old campaign." I take a long sip of my coffee.

"Well, what about a new logo? Like...make the Splash Wave green on all the drinks?"

We both make an uncomfortable face.

"I hate this. I am so blank." Ugh. So much for talking myself into a Monday Morning Reverie...so far the brainstorming was getting us nowhere.

"How are you doing? Or should I ask how James is doing?" Dez shifts the conversation just as I'm about to throw a pen.

I make a so-so sign with my hand.

"He's doing okay. On some level, I think it was an expected loss. I mean, his grandfather was ninety-three! It's just that it's never expected, you know?"

"And you feel helpless."

"Of course. Plus I keep thinking about something James said the night of the burial."

"What's that?"

"Well, he told me this great story about his grandfather, and then he wound it all up by saying that nothing is as important as being with your family. So now I feel like..."

"...you've got to fix it."

I shoot Dez an eye-roll and shake my head at the same time.

"What I was going to say was that now I feel like I totally have to do the Hanukkah thing."

"You're serious."

"Of course I am! I was serious when I first mentioned it to you."

"Rhon, I just feel like you're biting off a little more than you can chew with Hanukkah being the day after Christmas, not to mention you being the newest member of the family..." Dez shrugs and opens her hands expansively.

"Well, I could do Rosh Hashanah, but that's always at Aunt Bunny's." I'm thinking out loud.

"What do they usually do for Hanukkah?"

"You know, I don't know, I can't remember James really telling me..."

"Maybe they don't really do anything. My friend Judith always says that Hanukkah is for kids."

"Oh, please! That's like quitting Christmas the year you no longer believe in Santa!"

"I just think you should consider all the work that's going to go into this, and to consider that awful Jill eating the fruits of your labor..." Now it's Dez's turn to roll her eyes.

"Don't worry about Jill. Or the work. When have I ever been afraid of a little hard work?" I gesture towards the ever-growing pile of paper on my desk.

"Well, I know full well that once we wind you up..."

"The Energizer Bunny does not stand a chance!" I'm starting to get excited about the possibilities.

"Have you even discussed this with James?"

"What's there to discuss? I mean, he's the one who said that there's nothing as important..."

"I get it, I get it. The endless family diatribe." Dez seems to have no problem interrupting me. "Have you considered that this campaign is going to be due right around the same time you'll be belting out the Dreidel Song?" She points at the stuff we were just working on.

"Oh, please. We've got months. You know how it goes; we'll probably have two separate ideas by then, and we'll all be battling it out about which one to present."

"We hope. I just don't want to see you..."

"Overwhelmed?"

"Disappointed."

"Dez, you sound like the Prophet of Holiday Doom! Stop! If you don't want to see me overwhelmed, then please offer to help." I pause. "I know you're committed to the shelter on Christmas, but surely you can come help me out for Hanukkah...?" I go for the best puppy dog eyes I can possibly make, then shift from pleading and add in a little blinking action as if I'm flirting.

"You're ridiculous. Of course I'll help."

"I am so not ridiculous. I am..." I wave my hands.

"Desperately hoping you can pull it all off?" Dez suggests with a practiced wry grin.

"I am *excited!* Now, no more! We need to *Splash* into something..."

I see her give me an exquisite eye-roll and then we shift focus back to the drawing board.

As Mondays go...not bad.

Chapter Nine

By the time we sit down at Aunt Bunny and Uncle Ben's, I've had a glass or two of wine...just enough to have the warm fuzzies. I look at James's entire family seated around the gargantuan dining room table: Uncle Ben at the head with Aunt Bunny to his left, and Grandma seated prominently on his right. Vivian, Vlad, Ira and Jill are seated across from us, and there is another couple, George and Linda, seated right next to us. They are neighbors of Aunt Bunny and Uncle Ben and I know them only in passing. As I take another sip of wine, I decide to include them in my warm and fuzzy feeling.

I want to soak it all in: my first Rosh Hashanah as James's wife, the long table, decorated gaily with Autumn accents, that strong rush of emotion that only family can induce.

"L'Shana Tova! I'm so glad you can all be here," Uncle Ben announces. He gazes down the table and then picks up a tray with sliced apples, a small bowl of honey situated in the middle. He dips a piece of apple in the honey, thus beginning the ritual.

"Pass it down! Let's eat!" He laughs as he passes the platter down the row. Each member of the family takes their turn, passing the apples one to another.

"What a nice tradition. Ben, is there any significance to this?" Linda the Neighbor asks.

"It is..." Uncle Ben looks to Aunt Bunny for clarification.

"Ben, you are a Bad Jew!" She hits him playfully on the arm and turns towards Linda and George. "Sweetness in the year ahead."

"Fabulous, I'll take it!" George exclaims.

The group laughs as they commence eating the various foodstuffs displayed across the table. After much passing and thanking, Cousin Jill leans across the table and speaks directly to James.

"James, did you attend services today? I looked for you but didn't see you there."

James, in the midst of chewing, takes a quick drink and then shakes his head.

"No, Rhonda and I decided instead to go visit Grandpa's grave," James responds.

Vivian's head shoots up and she scowls across the table.

"And *whose* idea was that?" She says this to him but is looking at me.

"Mine, actually," James says. Eventually she looks from me to him. He holds his mother's gaze until she looks away.

I look from James to his mother, then start fiddling with the napkin in my lap. I'm about to refill my wine.

"I saw the cap you left there, James. Nice touch. Your grandfather would have liked it," Uncle Ben cuts in.

"Thanks, Uncle Ben. I thought so too."

There is a brief moment of silence and I decide to fill it.

"Everybody, I have something I would like to announce!" Call it liquid courage, but I figure it's as good a time as any.

I second guess myself as ten heads swing in my direction.

"For Land's Sake, please tell me you're not pregnant already!" Vivian bursts out with this.

"Vivian!" As Aunt Bunny shoots Vivian a warning look, Jill suddenly bursts into hysterics. Big tears are flowing down her cheeks almost instantly, and she looks as if she's about to launch into a full-blown panic attack. George and Linda look on in horror as if they wonder what they've just stepped into, and Jill continues blubbering and crying with no words coming out, only sounds that are akin to wildlife being killed. Ira gathers Jill in his arms and tries hushing her as the whole family looks on in alarm.

I am speechless. And horrified. What exactly just happened?

"Ssshh, sshh, honey, it's not true! Nobody's pregnant yet, Jilly..." He turns suddenly and addresses James and I with rancor. "You're not yet, are you?"

We manage to shake our heads in unison, shocked, as I continue to watch Jill carry on as if she is being murdered.

"I just wanted to..." I look at James but he's not helping.

"What! What is it?" Vivian again.

I swallow, take a deep breath, and try to force a normal voice while my eyes are still glued on Jill, who has begun to hyperventilate.

"I just wanted to announce that James and I will be hosting Hanukkah this year!" With that, I bang down my wine glass.

Vlad looks happy at the announcement until Vivian spits out, "Hanukkah?! Who does Hanukkah anymore?"

I shoot James a pleading look and he hesitates a moment, looking totally bewildered. A few beats later, he clears his throat and jumps in.

"We are. We thought it would be nice to have everyone over our place and..." Now he's stalled and returns the floor to me.

"...You know, just have some fun! Some food, some gifts, some dreidel games..." I try. I try to offer a smile, except I'm not exactly sure if anyone is listening or even looking in my direction.

Ira pulls a face as Jill begins an audible mantra through tears: "No babies, no babies, no babies..."

"Jilly, there are no babies yet. I promise, you'll have the first baby. Okay? Okay, Jill?" He shoots a look of contempt in the precise direction of both James and me. "You guys are going to have to wait. Okay?!"

"Ira, are you serious? Rhonda and I will have a baby when we're ready to..."

James is cut off by Jill blowing her nose as loud as a Shofar into Aunt Bunny's gold silk napkins. James looks to Uncle Ben to rescue him. Uncle Ben gets up and approaches Jill, as Linda and George stuff their mouths full of food. I see Uncle Ben remove Ira's arm and bend down to console the convulsive Jill. He whispers something in her ear and, after a minute, we hear Jill begin to laugh through tears. Uncle Ben continues to soothe Jill, and after another moment, we hear Jill snort loudly. She pushes away from the table and Ira and collapses into Uncle Ben. He pats her back and steers her away from everyone, in an effort to return her to some semblance of normal.

"Carry on, everyone. Jill and I will be right back." They exit the room and I look at James, still stunned at her reaction. He grabs my hand under the table and gives it a light squeeze.

Chapter Ten

We get in the door and I realize that I am still recovering from both the wine and the drama as I shrug off my jacket and hand it to James. I kick off my shoes a second later and begin padding directly into the kitchen. I hear James drop his keys in a dish on our hall table, then feel him come up behind me as I pour myself a huge glass of iced tea.

"So, when exactly did you decide that we were hosting Hanukkah?" He grabs my tea and finishes it off, then corners me with a quizzical expression.

"Aren't you excited?"

"I guess. I mean, I just wish you would have told me before you announced it to the entire family. Or asked me...you know, Rhonda, it would have been nice to have been included in your decision."

I grab the empty glass from his hand and pour myself another one.

I shrug.

"I thought you would love it! James, after that whole story you shared about Grandpa, I thought to myself, I said, '*How fabulous would it be to host a perfect Hanukkah?*' And then it sort of took on a life of its own...I mean, aren't you excited?" I gulp down the tea.

After he doesn't respond right away, I stare directly at him.

"Want some more?"

"I guess. I don't even know when Hanukkah is yet this year."

"It starts on the 26th." I've got this one down.

"Of December?" He looks surprised.

"Of course, silly!" I shake my head as I continue to drink more tea. "When is it ever not in December?"

"You do realize that's the day after Christmas?"

"Yes..." His point?

"Aren't we going to have everybody here for Christmas, too?"

"Of course! I just thought it would be nice to do a little something special for your family too...I only intend to host the first night, James...with drop-ins, of course."

"Drop-ins?"

"Well, I thought it would be nice to offer for anyone to drop in, you know, simply to light the candles, maybe sing a little song, whatever comes to mind...for the remainder of the nights."

"Drop-ins."

"James, really! Don't worry about anything...I've got it all under control. I promise, you are going to have the most perfect holiday!"

"I just don't want you to burn yourself out. Look…" He grabs me away from the counter and offers his lap for me to sit on. He swipes an errant hair off of my forehead and then concentrates on my face. "...it's been a pretty big year for us. We just had a wedding and a funeral, plus a major holiday today. We still have Thanksgiving to get through and then Christmas..."

"I know all that, James. I merely want things to be perfect! Don't you feel bad about Hanukkah always being edged out by Christmas? What would be the harm in really celebrating both holidays this year?"

"Look, I'm in...I just don't want to get so sucked in by the holiday madness that we can't find our way out again."

"It's going to be great." I give him a quick kiss. "Trust me."

Chapter Eleven

I'm staring at the whiteboard in front of me with all types of slogans scribbled across it in varying ink colors. My mind is going 150MPH even though I probably look frozen to the casual observer. Just as I'm about to get up to scribble something else on the board, my phone rings and I lean over to pick it up, not looking at the caller ID.

"Rhonda Golden."

"I always said you were my golden girl..."

"Daddy! How are you? Or should I ask, where are you?" I lean against my desk and smile.

"I'm home. My trip to Ohio was canceled, and I'm back a day early."

"Are you happy?"

"Happy? Happy is an understatement. I couldn't take another moment of introducing my replacement. SO, how's my girl?" Harry replies, happily shifting gears.

"I'm okay. I just had the holiday with James' family." I turn my back to the whiteboard and begin to move around the room in tight circles.

"So how did it go?"

"Okay. His cousin Jill is really preoccupied with having a baby, it seems...and Vivian is, well..." I am now drawing a line in the carpet with my shoe.

"A beast?" he offers with a guffaw.

"Daddy!" I try for an admonishing tone, but we both know he's right, not to mention funny as hell. I scribble another set of words on the board. He laughs.

"Listen sweetie, don't let her get to you. Anyway...I'm calling because I have tomorrow free and I would love to take you out to lunch, that is, if you're available."

"I'm available, and I would love to see you."

"Great. Then I'll pick you up at noon, your office?"

"You're on."

I hang up the phone with a smile and then sit back down on the edge of my desk, warily eyeing the whiteboard in front me on the easel.

A second later I hear a loud buzz and then Dez on the intercom.

"Rhon, what are you up to in there?"

I stare at the whiteboard and sigh.

"This is an order: Grab your purse, we are in desperate need of retail therapy!"

"You think that will help?" I chuck my pen.

"Of course it will! We're in advertising! Every time we futz around and shop, our minds are subliminally picking up great retail messaging," Dez insists.

"Well, I've got nothing. So I might as well."

"Meet you outside in five."

"You've got it."

Minutes later, we exit the building together and proceed to walk along the street, peering into shop windows as we go.

We hear a rendition of "It's The Most Wonderful Time of The Year" as we enter the first store and take that as our cue. From there, we start pulling apart a rack of glitzy holiday dresses, and eventually participate in a small fashion show of our own. After grabbing coffees we end up in an accessory store, plunging through a rack of purses. There's a guy standing in a display window, tearing down Autumn and putting up Christmas.

A few blocks down, we stumble upon a seasonal store, brightly lit, and already fully decorated for Christmas.

I motion to Dez. "Let's see if they've got any Hanukkah stuff."

"Rhonda, this is ridiculous! We haven't even had Halloween yet!"

"Come on, just come in with me and check it out." I steer her in, even as she groans.

"I love Christmas," I proclaim, as I take in the Winter Wonderland that's been built all around me.

"Come on, remember, you're looking for Hanukkah."

"Right." I look around and see a middle-aged salesman looking bored behind the counter. He's wearing a green vest and a red tie, so I figure it's a good sign.

"Hi there! I was wondering if you had any Hanukkah decorations?" He barely glances up and then points to a far corner of the store.

"Back there."

Dez and I share a look. So much for a good sign.

"Okay. Thanks." I take a deep breath and then tramp down a long aisle filled to overflowing with everything Christmas: stockings, wreaths, light displays and accessories. When I get to the end of the aisle, I see a single pot holder in the shape of a Menorah hanging all by itself. I look around, behind, up and down, then to Dez.

"You think that's all they have?" I'm a bit surprised.

"Well...it is a little early..." Dez tries.

"Yeah, but look at all the Christmas stuff they have!" I indicate the piles of stuff surrounding me at every turn. I refuse to believe that's all they have.

"I think...I think that's just the way it is, Rhonda." She shrugs and makes a face.

"Well, that's silly!" I am incensed.

"Rhon, you know you can't make Hanukkah Christmas..."

"I don't intend to make Hanukkah Christmas! I just...do you see the disparity here? Don't you think they should have a little more...something? Anything?"

"I do. But they don't. So let's get the potholder and call it a day." Dez points to the lone potholder.

"I don't want the measly potholder."

I do a full 360 degree turn in the aisle.

"Hold on."

I then decide to confront the salesman, who is now listening to an ipod and reading a magazine. He doesn't acknowledge me. At all. I decide to start waving my hands in front of his face as if ushering in a plane.

He finally removes his earbuds and shoots me an annoyed look.

"Yeah?"

"Is that all the Hanukkah merchandise you have?"

"Yeah."

And with that, he goes back to his ipod.

Just as I'm about to implode, Dez steers me gently away from the counter and towards the exit to the Winter Wonderland. As we leave and head back towards the office, I find that I am shaking my head in tune with my steps.

"I'm just going to have to try online."

"That's a great idea, Rhon. I'm sure you'll find tons of stuff online."

"I hope so. I can't believe James has had to deal with this his entire life!"

"I hate to break it you, toots, but I don't think James cares." Dez states this as if it is fact.

"You don't?" I am incredulous.

"I don't think anybody cares about the holidays as much as you do."

"I just think you hate the holidays."

"I'm surprised you don't."

I take a deep breath and continue to stomp towards work. Desiree bites her lip.

"That's probably why we're such good friends."

I look quizzically at Dez.

"We balance each other out. Now, back to work!" Dez pushes me in front of her and we walk through the revolving door back into our building.

Chapter Twelve

I'm meeting Dad for lunch today, and just as I'm about to start making my napkin into various pieces of cruise ship dining art, he appears, his signature grin plastered across his face.

"Well, if it isn't my favorite ad exec!" Dad exclaims as he crushes me in an awkward hug.

"Ah, Daddy! You are not allowed to mention work right now, or I will be completely unable to eat." I finish off the hug with a kiss on each cheek and then motion for him to sit. The server comes by and offers each of us a menu, and as we settle in, Dad loosens up his tie.

"Well, let me know what I can mention. I'm not sure if you want to talk about the whole Hanukkah thing either." He rolls his eyes.

"Oh, it's a Hanukkah THING now?! Whatever happened to having a holiday celebration?" I give him an eye roll back.

"Holiday, thing, whatever. You know all that stuff doesn't really jazz me...are we ordering?"

I nod my head, but inside I'm dying. I feel this overwhelming urge to burst into tears and in an effort to stem the tide of emotion that's suddenly swelling inside of me, I lift up my napkin once again and refold it. Then I place it back on my lap and look at him as he peruses the menu, seemingly unaware of what he just did to me.

After a moment's silence, he places the menu on his plate and then looks directly at me.

"What's up, Miss Golden?" He's fidgeting too. I can see it under the table.

"I just want..." I make a gesture and then slap my hands on the table. "I just want to create a really fabulous holiday season. You know? I want James to enjoy his holiday as much as we enjoy ours...well, as much as we used to...and I want my mother-in-law to..."

"To what, Rhonda? Sweetie, listen," he sighs and then takes my hand in his across the menus. "I've met and dealt with a lot of women in my life just like Vivian. Her problems have nothing to do with you, I assure you."

"I know...you know, I thought about this a lot, and I just want to create a perfect memory."

"And I think that's great! You should." He releases my hand and sighs. "I want you to be happy, Rhonda, and if that's what's going to make you happy...then I'm all for it. I only wish your mother was around to help with the baking."

He leans back in his chair and looks for the waiter.

I find myself fighting back tears again, and he pretends not to see. He motions towards the server, then glances my way.

"You ready?"

Chapter Thirteen

"So how's it going?" James asks as he wanders into the kitchen and takes a look over my shoulder.

"I don't know!" I hear myself whining but am unable to stop. In one deft motion, I take off the *MERRY CHRISMUKKAH* apron that I've been wearing and point to the lump of dough that's been giving me a hard time.

"It looks...well, how is it supposed to look?" He peers curiously over the top of his beer and looks between me and the dough.

"I'm not sure." The entire countertop is encrusted in flour and I feel flour all over me, even in my hair. "I just thought it was supposed to be bigger...I refrigerated this thing almost three days ago!"

"Well, give it a whirl, and if it doesn't work out, you can always buy some."

"Buy some!" I shake my head as if this is preposterous. Then I try another tack. "Oh! James, do you think your Mom might know something about..."

He waves his hand to cut me off as a cheer goes up from the football game currently on the TV. He then pumps his fist in the air and gives out an excited yell.

"Rhonda, my mother never made any kind of bread. Don't kill yourself; just buy some bread the day before, and everyone will love it." He begins to wander away.

"The day before is Christmas! Nothing will be open, James. I just...well, I've got time to get it right."

Unfortunately, I realize I did not get it right as I lift a completely flat, slightly smoking, obviously ruined challah bread from the oven about 45 minutes later.

"Ugh!" I take the bread and toss it on top of the stove as if it contains poison, then allow myself to disintegrate into tears.

I decide I need a cappuccino.

A few sips in, I put my determined face on, grab my coffee, and fire up my laptop.

I type into Google: "Make a Great Hanukkah?"

The search engine gives me a bunch of options. I rub my hands together and flex my wrists, as if diving into a Hanukkah pool. The first site I click on reads:

SHALOM AND WELCOME...to a celebration of the Jewish holiday of CHANUKAH!

"James! James, how did you spell Hanukkah growing up?" I'm suddenly alarmed.

I hear something garbled in response coming from the general area of the bedroom.

"James? Can you hear me? What are you doing in there?"

"Looking for my ski gloves," James calls out.

"Wouldn't your ski gloves be by your skis?" I look over my shoulder and see him enter the room, his hair rumpled and a frustrated expression on his face.

"One would think so. Anyway, what were you asking me?"

"I wanted to know how you spelled Hanukkah growing up."

"With an H."

"Okay, because I want to send out the invitations with the spelling your family will be familiar with." Surely sending out invitations will be easier than the challah massacre.

"You called me in here for that?"

"Oh, that and I wanted to know if you sang." I'm starting to brew with ideas now.

"Sang? As in songs?" He looks bewildered.

"Yes. A lot of Jewish families sing Hanukkah songs. Oh! Remember the one from grade school?"

His face is blank, so I launch into a fairly horrible rendition of:

HANUKKAH! HANUKKAH!
SEVEN DAYS, EIGHT NIGHTS!
HANUKKAH! HANUKKAH!
MADE MENORAH LIGHT!
HANUKKAH! HANUKKAH!
MADE THE DREIDEL SPIN!
HANUKKAH! HANUKKAH!
EVERYONE JOIN IN!!

I stand up and applaud myself.

James, however, has an appalled look etched on his face and cannot move. He stands there utterly speechless.

"James, don't tell me you don't remember that song!"

"I have never heard that song before in my life." And he looks horrified.

"Well, we'll just have to add it to our list then. I can't believe you've never heard that song..." I mean, I learned it in grade school, and I'm not Jewish, but I still remember it by heart.

"What list?"

"The list of Hanukkah carols, well...I guess they wouldn't be called carols for Hanukkah, but...you get the picture."

"Rhonda, I know some Jews that sing at Passover, but my family never even did that. I just don't know how many takers you're going to have on the singing front."

"Well, Jill will sing with me."

"Jill seems to be in the midst of a nervous breakdown."

"Then I'm sure I can get Ira..."

"I think Ira will be too busy helping Jill not commit suicide."

"I noticed he's..." I trail off.

"Probably the reason Jill can't get pregnant?" James snickers.

"James! Don't say that!" I admonish him with a wide-eyed look and a light tap on the arm. "One day that could be us."

"That could never be us, because you're at least somewhat normal."

"Thanks, I think." I turn my back to him and continue scouring the Internet for Hanukkah ideas. "Do me a favor?" I want to grab him before he dives back into the closet.

"Fill the printer up with paper before you go. I think I'm going to need it." I smile to myself.

Chapter Fourteen

I'm full of turkey and overflowing with boxes. It's Thanks-giving weekend and I just had James pull all of our Holiday decorations out of the attic. There are boxes and cartons piled all around the living room, brandishing labels such as: *Lights, Ornaments, Etc.* I'm about to dive in but decide to put on a little mood music first...something energizing. James is glued to the couch as I begin poring through our CD rack. After several moments of this, I lean across James, grab the remote, and mute the TV.

"Hey!"

"Hey! Did you ever notice that there's no such thing as Hanukkah music?!" I decide I'm outraged.

He then tries to dive over the coffee table in order to steal the remote back from me. I shoot him a look and although he has the remote back, he sets it gently on the table with the sound still muted.

"What are you talking about?"

"That's the problem! There's tons of Christmas music! Virtual truckloads!" I begin pulling CD's out of the rack one by one. "Even animated characters have their own Christmas albums!" I shove *A Charlie Brown Christmas* by the Vince Guaraldi Trio right under his nose. "But there's no Hanukkah music! None! Initially, I thought maybe we just didn't have any...but I looked online and there's *none.*"

"Well, as I have been repeatedly trying to tell you...Hanukkah is not Christmas..." James is patient, far more patient than the crazy woman standing beside him.

"Look! Look at this! Barbra Streisand has not one, but several Christmas albums! Neil Diamond, look! They're traitors, all of them!"

"Rhonda, I feel the need to remind you at this point that you're not Jewish."

"I'm boycotting them! I won't listen to them until they put out something with a great big Hanukkah bow on it!" I declare.

"Rhonda, you can boycott them all you want...but you already own the CD's, so..."

"Well, what I am supposed to play on Hanukkah...the *Jazz Singer* soundtrack?! Maybe I can whip out a ham too and your cousin Ira can tear at his clothes! Do you think that would be a good idea?!"

James begins to chuckle. He puts the sound back on the TV and shakes his head.

"Rhonda, I think you should call the Israeli consulate..."

I'm not listening.

I turn my back to him and begin noisily clacking the CD's back into their places on the shelf.

"Forget it. You just don't get it."

"I get it. I do..."

"No. You don't."

Chapter Fifteen

I tap my pen several hundred times before I give up and toss it across my desk, annoyed by life in general.

I sigh to no one, then get up and take in my Christmas paraphernalia: the blinking lights adorning all four corners of my desk, the wreath I hang on the inside of my door, and the table-top tree that is situated on my bookshelf.

I wish for my mother.

"Oh, Mom..." I'm whispering out loud, and as I begin to communicate with my mother, I feel a lone tear slide down my face. "I'm stuck at work. Really stuck. I'm supposed to be coming up with a new campaign slogan for *Splash* Beverages and I find myself totally blank." I clear my throat and ask, "Pray for me?"

I sigh again, then step away from my desk, turning my back to the whiteboard still perched nearby. I hustle over to the window and pull the blinds shut tight, and continue talking to my Mom.

"And I wish I could find some gelt. Remember how we used to fill a bowl in the front hallway with chocolate Christmas bells?

Well, I want to do the same thing for Hanukkah...except gelt, of course, and I can't find any big bags, and I don't want to buy a thousand individual pieces and break them all up. And..." I can't go on, and as the tears begin coursing down my cheeks, I start trying to take deep breaths but manage to sound as if I am doing some weird form of Lamaze. I rip a few tissues out of a holiday-themed tissue box, then continue. "...and I need you. My baking sucks! I hate doing this without you! This whole *very important* year I've been doing it without you, and..." I pause for a second and look at the ceiling. "I miss you, Mom."

I sniff hard, then cross the room to fix my face. I know I need to focus and get back to work, but I feel like I need a coffee break. Just as I'm about to go find Dez, the door bangs closed behind me.

"Hey! I called you twice!" Dez sails into the room, dancing with a cappuccino in her hand. She is grinning from ear to ear as she shrugs off her scarf and sits down, humming *Jingle Bells*.

Perfect timing.

"To what do I owe this pleasure? And did I just hear you humming *Jingle Bells?*"

Dez laughs, hesitates as she takes me in for a second, then practically accosts me.

"Who's your best friend?"

"You are. But that's not news. And that doesn't tell me why you're caroling."

"Tell me: Who's the best Hanukkah Elf...ever?"

"I'm assuming you." I look her up and down and then lean towards her until we are directly eye to eye, "Spill."

"Sit!"

I sit.

"Okay! So remember my mother's crazy neighbors, Casey and Casey?" Dez looks like she's got something up her sleeve.

"Of course! The couple who almost named their twins Taylor and Taylor!" I guffaw.

Desiree nods and shakes her head at the same time.

"Well, those two jackasses are finally getting divorced."

"What did they end up naming their twins again?"

"Jack and...wait for it..." Dez makes a "stop" signal with one hand, as the realization dawns on me.

"Jill?!" I'm shouting now.

"What else? Anyway, we are sliding off topic here. Focus! I was out at my mother's the other day and I ran into Casey while I was walking in from the driveway."

"Which one?"

"The woman."

"Okay. Go ahead."

"So we shoot the breeze for what seems like forever, and then all of the sudden, she's crying her eyes out, leaning over the fence, clutching the shrubs, and making a horrific little bit of a scene," Dez waves her hand as if this woman's misery is not worth delving into.

"I get it. You got caught. I'm just not putting together how this makes you the best Hanukkah Elf ever."

"I'm getting to it. Did I ever tell you what Casey does for a living?"

"Which one?"

"The guy."

"I don't think so."

"Well, he's some sort of Concession Supply guy...he rents

out and sells all kinds of stuff for parties and events...popcorn machines, all kinds of nostalgia...and guess what Casey the Female wants to unload prior to the big D?" Dez is practically beaming at this point.

"A cotton candy machine?" I have no idea what made me guess that.

"No! HANUKKAH INFLATABLES!" Dez proceeds to jump up and down.

"Dez, do you mean like..." My mind is racing.

"For the yard! You know how most people have that whole blow-up Santa thing that they put up every year and the little snowmen and all that junk?"

"Well, I don't consider it junk..." I think I have two.

"You know what I mean! She's got this Hanukkah Bear, it's an eleven foot tall airblown inflatable, and it's just too much, Rhonda, the bear has a yarmulke on, and..." She's gesticulating wildly at this point.

"Can you get it?"

"Get it? I got it!"

"YOU DID?!" Oh...Joy to the World!

"I got that and an inflatable Menorah that you are just going to love...for a fraction of the cost! Rhon, they're looking to liquidate, you know, so I had to jump on it. Now, tell me...who do you love?"

"You!" I begin jumping up and down now too. I then smother Dez in a huge bear hug. "Oh, Dez! Thank you! Thank you so much!"

Dez embraces me, then pats my back, and exhales over my shoulder.

"I know how important this is to you."

Chapter Sixteen

"Do you think it's too much?" I am standing at the edge of our yard, looking towards the house. On one side of the yard is the humongous Hanukkah bear, and next to it is a halfway inflated Menorah that keeps listing to one side. The opposite side of the lawn boasts an inflatable Santa, Frosty the Snowman, candy cane stakes, reindeer, and Snoopy, dressed in a Santa hat, putting a letter into a decorated mailbox. There are snowflakes glittering in the windows.

There is silence save for the fans located somewhere inside the holiday inflatables. James looks perplexed.

"It looks like we're at war." He splays his arms open and pulls a face.

"War?" I make the same face. "What do you mean?"

"Well, we've got Hanukkah on one side and Christmas on the other..."

"Do you think we should alternate?" Now I'm perplexed.

"I don't know. I know this is important to you; the problem is that I don't really know how it should look."

We stand there gazing at the display in silence as our nosy neighbor, Celia, peers over the hedge.

"Oh, very politically correct! You two sure you don't want to hang a Kwanzaa banner in the middle somewhere?" she cackles, and disappears behind the hedge.

We look at each other and suddenly, we just start cracking up. We're laughing so hard we're doubling over into the street. After a minute, we catch our breath and James calls a time-out.

"Babe, you're the one who's done all this stuff your whole life. How's it supposed to look?"

"Not like this."

And we collapse into laughter once again.

Chapter Seventeen

I decide to hang glass Christmas ornaments in between each candle on an already ornate Menorah. It may be too much, so I lean back and give it a more critical eye.

Not too much.

I turn up the Christmas music and then decide to focus on the mantel above the fireplace. I put my three wooden letters: J-O-Y right smack dab in the middle.

"I think it needs a little more holly," I say to myself as I delve into a nearby box and begin pulling out various greens with bright red berries attached. As I pull them out carefully, some of the berries detach and roll onto the floor. Just as I start trying to catch them, the doorbell rings.

"What the...?"

I see James standing outside the front door, leaning on the bell, a glove in his mouth, and what appears to be a heavy box in his hands. I scramble towards the door and open it up with a flourish.

"Did you forget your keys?"

"Hey, honey!" He says this with the glove still in his mouth and then puts the box down with a THWUMP. A second later he rips the glove out of his mouth. "I just left them in the car. But then I had the box, and since I saw you through the window... finishing up?" He peers over my shoulder into the living area, all while hanging up his coat and planting a quick kiss on my forehead.

"Trying to finish. What's that?" I indicate the box.

"Oh! That, my dear, is insurance."

"Insurance?"

"That all will be merry and bright..." He opens the flaps and starts handing me one bottle after another.

"Kahlua, Bailey's, almond liqueur, a nice gin, some vodka, and of course, a bottle of wine."

I'm now loaded down with bottles.

"For Christmas? Hanukkah?" I begin to transfer each one back into the box.

"Both. Gin for your Dad; a little wine for Uncle Ben. And I figured if my mother steps out of line, well...a Toasted Almond usually puts her right back in."

"I didn't know your mother liked Toasted Almonds."

"Well, her and Vlad are known to down a Toasted Almond from time to time."

"I think that's great. You're taking care of the logistics while I'm finishing with the aesthetics."

"Exactly! So what else have you been up to?"

"Just putting the finishing touches on all of the decor. I feel done, does it look done to you?" I make a sweeping gesture with my arm, taking in an overflowing Christmas tree laden with all forms of lights and ornaments; the mantel, coffee table, and bookshelves, transformed into a Christmas village; stockings hung by the chimney with care; as well as several different styles of Menorahs peppered throughout the room.

"I think the room has never looked better! By the way, where did you get all of this stuff?" He looks around slowly and takes it in, as if noticing it all for the very first time.

"Well..." I find myself blushing, but I grab him by the arm and move him closer to the tree. "See this?" I indicate an old-fashioned Snoopy ornament dangling from a branch.

He nods.

"I've been collecting these ever since I was little. I always loved Christmas, and I always knew that one day I would have my own house, and that I would want to really decorate it."

"Like when you walk into Macy's, and all the trees are decorated just so?"

I shrug. "Sort of. Don't get me wrong, I love the trees and all the decorations they put up at the department stores. It's just that sometimes they look too perfect. I always wanted my tree and all of my holiday stuff to reflect me...even if it's not color-coordinated."

"Well, from a guy who has never once had a live tree in his house...I can tell you that I think you've done a fabulous job so far."

"You think?"

"I think."

James leans in to kiss me, and I slowly wrap my hands around his neck and pull him in closer, kissing him deeper. We continue kissing with the Christmas tree as backdrop, until James pulls me towards the couch, where we proceed to undress each other slowly.

Chapter Eighteen

"Help me, Rhonda!" Dez peeks her head into my office with this ridiculousness.

"Gee, I've never heard that one before." I scowl at her, as much as I can scowl at Dez, and then I motion her in and indicate the three-ring binder I've been poring over for inspiration.

I shake my head and feel my Christmas ball earrings bang gently against my cheek. If I keep doing this, they're going to have to come off.

"What've you got?" I sigh this rather than say it. "Not much. I'm still dreaming about recycling the old campaign. UGH!" Dez slumps down in the chair opposite.

"Look, I agree. I don't know what else to add here. Does anyone on the team have anything even remotely decent?"

Dez shakes her head no.

"Well, Ramon has some great artwork so far; he's drawn a tree with all the different *Splash* beverages hanging off the branches... but he needs something to write on it, or under it..." she shrugs.

"This is going to sound so cliché, but I feel like everything that needs to be said about recycling and going green has already been said."

"I agree. And get this: Lola just found out that Artie is going to be away from the 23rd of December on..."

"Great. Does that mean he expects us to wrap the whole thing up for him?" I moan.

"With a pretty little bow."

"Oh, bow! You remind me...I need a few more of those little stick-on bows." I jot it down on my ever-growing list.

Desiree begins playing with a wind-up Santa on my desk.

"Yes, how is the HolidayPalooza going?"

"It's really starting to come together! I have the entire interior of the house decorated, the outside is...lit...and well, I just found out that my mother-in-law is a coffee fiend."

"And the coffee is important how?"

"Well, now I know what to get her for Hanukkah! Dez, I had no real idea before. I mean, I knew she liked cigarettes, but buying someone cigarettes is like giving them cancer, so..."

Dez grins wickedly. "So you've decided against cancer?"

I throw a candy cane pen in her direction. Dez ducks and laughs a raucous laugh.

"So you didn't ask me what I did this weekend." She mentions as she reaches for the pen on the floor.

"Oh, sorry Dez! What did you do?"

"I met someone." She is swinging her leg now, leaning back in the chair, trying hard not to smile.

"Someone who?!"

"Someone named Jack."

"And?!"

"And...I don't know!" She is smiling now, a full-out grin that reaches to her eyes.

"You know the rules. Spill!" I order her.

"Well, I can only tell you what I know so far. I know that he's thirty-seven, new to the area, and supercute."

"Where did you meet him? When?"

"I met him...drumroll please..."

I initiate a drumroll...

"I met him at the shelter."

"No!"

"Yes!"

"Seriously? Was he there to volunteer? And why am I just hearing about this now?!"

"No, he was actually there as a contractor. Not sure if I told you, but they're fixing part of the roof, and he was in and out all day Saturday. I noticed him right away, but we didn't talk until late afternoon, and then we just couldn't stop talking! I felt like SUCH a teenager; Rhon, I think they invented the word *swoon* for situations just like this...!"

"Oh my God, Dez! I'm so happy to hear that! So, what happened? Are you going to see him again?"

Desiree arches one eyebrow.

"Coffee. Tomorrow."

"I love it!" I get up and dance over to Dez, pulling her to her feet and twirling her around the room. Dez is laughing and telling me to stop.

"Don't get too excited. Yet."

"I just think it's so great!" With that, we're suddenly interrupted by Artie barging through the door. He takes in our posture and then makes a curious face.

"I do so hope you ladies are talking about a *pitch* for a certain beverage company that's *'so great!'* He clasps his hands together in a shoddy imitation of me, and stares us both down, one at a time. I clear my throat and Dez begins to speak.

"Actually, Artie, I do think we're on the edge. The cusp. The verge of---"

Artie softens his pose.

"Something fabulous?" he suggests.

"We hope!" I offer.

"Well, then, I'll leave you two. I just popped by to let you know that I'm leaving for Aspen on the 19th."

"The 19th?!" Dez and I say this in concert.

"I heard you were leaving on the 23rd." Desiree jumps in with this next.

"I was, but now I have a marvelous opportunity that I must take advantage of..." He peers in the direction of the whiteboard as I purposely step directly in front of his view.

"...besides, I trust that you lovely ladies will have the new campaign all sewn up by the time the champagne bottles are being uncorked and the calendar page is turned."

"We are so on it, Artie. Don't worry! Just get out there and have a blast. We'll see you in the New Year!" I begin steering Artie towards the door. Artie stops in his tracks, and does the little hand gesture he's famous for: "Look-Eye."

"You two have a few weeks left to shine, and I expect *sparkly* from this team!" he announces with a flourish. We continue to reassure Artie and gently push him out the door. Once the door is shut, I break out into a no-holds-barred grin.

"Dez! I so do not care about that! The campaign will come... what I'm really excited about is that now you have enough time to get to know Jack and bring him to my house for Hanukkah!"

"Slow down, you! I know you too well, and when you have that kind of smile on your face you're positively dangerous!"

"Of course I am. Dez, this Holiday Season is about to be the best one yet!" I'm convinced.

Chapter Nineteen

I figure I've done enough damage to my credit card as I begin to exit the department store chock-full of bags, both hands full. Of course, that's precisely when Mariah Carey decides to burst into "All I Want For Christmas Is You."

God, I love that ringtone.

I transfer all my bags to one hand and dive into the endless abyss that is my purse. I manage to navigate the revolving door, but just as I snatch up my phone, I bang into somebody coming towards me.

"Oooh, sorry!" My response is automatic, but then I look up and say, "Oh my God, it's Tad!"

A blush instantly creeps up my face as I realize that I said that out loud. I stand there a moment and stare until I hear the ring tone abruptly cut off, the caller sent to voice mail.

"It is Tad! And, as I live and breathe! Rhonda, you look just as good as I remember! No...better. So, how've you been?" He responds by taking me in, every aspect of me, and grinning like an idiot. People are swarming around us now, so I motion him to one side.

"I'm good. Real good. I was just...finishing up some holiday shopping..." I indicate my bags and give him what I hope is a warm and welcoming smile, save for the crimson cheeks.

"Oh, please! Don't tell me you've given in to the whole 'holiday shopping' thing, too! It's Christmas, Rhonda, remember what Pastor Craig used to say?" Tad has a way of talking that fills the entire space around us.

"Let's keep the Christ in Christmas." I nod my head and smile again.

"Exactly! See how that old youth group stuff just sort of sticks around inside your head?" he guffaws. I take a deep breath.

"I agree, Tad...it's just that I am shopping for more than one holiday."

"Oh?"

"Yes. Yeah, I...am shopping for Hanukkah as well as Christmas."

"Oh, co-workers? That's nice."

"No, it's actually for my husband's family. We're having a great big Hanukkah celebration at our house this year."

"Really?" He looks put off by this information, as his eyes flick briefly towards my ring hand. Then comes the awkward recovery. "Well, hey, I think that's great. I...ah, I guess maybe the youth group lessons didn't stick so well with you, hah? Ha! Ha... Ah hah, well...but you know, whatever works for you. I think that's great, you know Rhonda, it's great if you guys can make it work." He clears his throat.

I can't believe I ever thought he was gorgeous.

"Thanks, Tad. We are...very happy." I'm mildly confused by his reaction, but I wait a beat and decide to dive in anyway. "So what are you up to?

I haven't heard anything from the old youth group grapevine, so..."

"Well, believe it or not, I am the Youth Services Minister at the new church! Yes, I am newly appointed and ready to serve!" He makes a weird saluting motion with his hand, while I try hard not to flinch.

"It's been a good time had by all," he continues. "In fact, we're doing a Tree Decorating contest this Saturday. Our theme is, 'JESUS is the Light of the World!'" He is positively beaming, looking off into the middle distance. "Why don't you guys stop by? You can see the new addition, and string a few lights...unless, of course, your husband would be uncomfortable..."

"I think James would be fine. Listen, can I let you know?" I indicate the packages that are weighing down my arms.

"Oh, sure! Of course. I mean, let me give you my card, and..." He extends a multicolored business card, written in graffiti font.

I take it without a word.

"I made it cool, you know, for the kids." Now he's blushing.

"Of course! Well, I'll let you know. It was great seeing you. Take care."

"Oh, and Rhonda...if I don't see you...Merry Christmas!"

"You too, Tad. A Very Merry!" I turn on my heel and walk away from him, dialing Dez madly as I shift packages and make my way towards the car.

"Hey! What was that all about, I was calling to---"

"Dez! You are not going to believe who I just ran into!"

"Santa."

"Dez, be serious. I'm a TAD bit surprised that you can't make a serious guess." I try not to giggle.

"That was a serious guess."

"Well, then I'm a TAD bit upset that you still can't figure it out!" I say this while shoving packages into the car, my scarf getting stuck. I unravel it, waiting for her to make the connection.

"Oh my God, did you just run into Youth Group Tad?!"

"You got it. Took you a minute."

"Where? And what does he look like?"

"One guess."

"Preppy."

"You got it. He's still gorgeous, but he *looks like* a Youth Minister."

"Is he a youth minister?" Dez inquires in a voice reserved for spreading salacious gossip.

"Apparently! He seemed so...I don't know..."

"Uptight?"

"I guess. Just strange. Anyway, why were you calling me?"

"Oh, I was dying and I desperately needed you to call an ambulance, but I'm fine now, no worries."

"Dez?"

"I needed to tell you that I am in lust."

"Not love?"

"Not yet."

"Sounds good. So when do we get to meet him?"

"Back off, Mrs. Claus! I will introduce him when the time is right. I just want to swoon a little..."

"You've used that word twice this week," I feel the need to point out.

"I know! Isn't that great?"

"It is! Look, I've got to go...I've got to get home and try a new recipe, all while wrapping some gifts and trying to decide what kind of table linens I'm going to use."

"Okay, call me when you're almost done. I'm bringing over a bottle of wine and forcing you to chill."

"I don't have time to chill!"

"We'll make time. Gotta go. Love you!"

"Love you too."

I'm humming "Here Comes Santa Claus" the whole way home, excited to see my house all lit up on approach.

Sometimes it really is the simple things.

I convince myself I will focus more on the simple things.

However when I approach my house, I find that all the lights are off outside, and the inflatables dead on the front lawn.

What the...?

I troop inside, calling for James. The house is pitch-black, and I hear a muffled groan come from somewhere near the couch. After stepping into the kitchen, I set down all the packages, turn on the stove, and then make my way into the living room, flicking on lights as I go. I find James sprawled on the couch, in a pair of sweats, and old college tee, and a baseball cap.

"James! Have you been lying here all afternoon?" I look at James with alarm, as he takes a full minute to stretch and yawn.

"Yeah, hey babe. Did you bring home any food?"

"Food! James, are you serious? I told you I was going to try out that new pasta dish tonight! I want to give it a quick run-through before the holiday." I begin picking up the remnants of a snack and a dirty mug off the coffee table.

"Okay, how long?" James mutters this as he grabs for a throw pillow. He situates the pillow under his head and turns, all eyes on the television.

"How long until what? Dinner?" Now I'm annoyed. I make it clear by stalking over to the Christmas tree and stomping on the floor tapper, which lights up the tree and all of the window lights. "And I can't believe you didn't turn on my lights! I mean, it's only a week until Christmas and Hanukkah! Why even put up the lights if we're not going to turn them on?"

"I forgot."

"You forgot? You have a living tree in your house, James! How on Earth can you forget?!" I raise my hands in exasperation and then stomp back into the kitchen.

"Look, Rhon, it's been a helluva week. I just needed time to veg out, that's all." He rises up from the couch and then looks over the back of it, watching me unpack the bags.

I give him the evil eye.

"All I know is that I would love to have some time to VEG! But I have gifts to wrap, and recipes to taste test, and apparently... lights to put on, because you can't even TAP THE TAPPER!" I say this, indicating the little gadget on the floor where you tap your foot and it illuminates the entire scene. I hear myself and I realize that I must sound like a raving lunatic, but I'm way past caring. I am trying to pry a tag off of a bottle and getting more frustrated by the minute.

"And whose fault is that?" He's up off the couch now, and glaring at me from across the room.

"What are you talking about?" I put down the bottle and place my hands on both hips.

"What am I talking about?!" He makes a flailing gesture with his hands. "I'm talking about this! About everything! So I forgot to turn on the freaking lights! Who cares? Do you think the neighbors are going to come up and tap on the door and say, '*Mr and Mrs. Golden? It's dark outside and we noticed that the blowups have blown down and your windows are not illuminated!*' DO YOU THINK that we might receive neighborhood demerits?!? Really, Rhonda, can you give a guy a break here?" And he stands there with his hands wide-open and then slaps his sides for emphasis.

I'm crying now, and there's no way I can explain to him the myriad of emotions coursing through my veins.

"I just hate an unlit tree."

"Of course you do. You know what, Rhon? You've got a whole boatload of stuff that you've got to take care of...so I'm just going to go." He starts heading toward the coat closet.

"Go?! Where are you going?" What the hell just happened?

"I'm going to go have a glass of wine with Uncle Ben. Okay? I'll be out of your way in just a minute."

He opens the door as he jams sneakers on his feet, grabs his keys and a jacket, and slams the door as he leaves.

I sit down in the nearest chair and burst into tears all over again. The phone rings as I watch him pull out of the driveway, and I hear an animated voice on the answering machine offering me a free trial for something.

I ignore the call and cross the room to throw on a light switch.

Outside, all the lawn ornaments come to life.

Chapter Twenty

I'm on my second glass of wine, quietly contemplating my third as I gaze out the window, my legs tucked up underneath me. Dez is right across from me, finishing up a call. The minute she closes her cell and smiles over at me, I instantly collapse into huge sobs.

"Aw, Rhon, come on sweetie. You guys just had a little fight, that's all. He'll be back soon, and then I'll leave, and you guys will be totally back in love before daybreak."

"It's just not...not...first year married...what I pictured..." I'm making no sense.

"It's going to be okay. Come here." She pats the seat next to her. When I fail to join her, she places her wine glass carefully down on the coffee table, making sure to put a coaster underneath.

This is a true friend.

Next she moves over to me, removing my wine glass from my hand.

Maybe not such a pal.

Then Dez places it on a matching coaster.

Slightly redeemed.

When Dez leans in to envelop me in a huge hug, I am still sobbing, making my way to the dry heaves.

"Men just don't get it. We put in a lot of effort, us ladies...well, you do anyway...and they just don't get that all we want is a little bit of appreciation."

"I want a lot of appreciation!" I sniffle, then swipe my face with the back of my hand, knowing that my makeup is now irreparably smeared. Dez offers me a tissue, which I take, then blow my nose so loud that Dez begins to chuckle.

I look at Dez and laugh through tears.

"I'm being ridiculous, aren't I?"

"A little."

"I just want everything to be perfect. I want to look back on this time and realize that I gave James the best holiday ever, the first year we got married!"

"Well, Rhonda, I think you're doing all that you can and then some. I mean, look at those cookies!"

Desiree makes a gesture towards the kitchen island, which is laden with brilliant blue and silver cookies, each one representing a different Hanukkah icon.

"They did come out pretty good," I sniff again and then get up to survey my work. "I think it's important to have Hanukkah-specific cookies. Everybody makes Christmas cookies this time of year, what's so imaginative about that?"

"That's the spirit!" Dez toasts to this.

I grab another few tissues out of a nearby box and blow my nose again. I need to take a few deep breaths and regroup.

"And you liked the pasta?" I turn towards the trial run.

"What's there not to like?"

"Thanks! Oh, thank you Dez! I feel better already! Can you help me pack up these cookies? I found some great Hanukkah tins online."

"Gladly. Do you want them---"

We are interrupted by the ringing of the phone. I look at Dez and Dez motions for me to grab it.

"He's probably calling you to apologize..."

I fluff my hair, take a deep breath, and answer on the fourth ring.

"Hey! Is James there?"

"No, I'm sorry, he's not here right now." I'm not quite sure who it is at first, my mind flicking through different characters that may match the voice on the other end of the phone. "Who's this?"

"His cousin Dave. Is this Rhonda?"

Who else? "Oh, yes! I remember you from the wedding. How have you been?"

I begin hearing what sounds like sirens in the background, and he seems to be speaking to someone else.

"Stand by."

Is he talking to me?

Static, then I hear David again. "I'm coming into town soon and I just wanted to touch base with Jay."

Jay?

"Got it. Well, why don't you come over here on the 26th? We're having a Hanukkah celebration and I'm sure James would love to see you..." I'm cut off by a blaring sound and a laugh in the background.

"That'll work. What time?"

"I don't know, about three-ish...anytime, really. I'll let him know you called. Should I have him call you back or would you like his cell?"

"No, we're good. 10-4 and I'll see you then."

I replace the phone and shoot Dez a look.

"I gather that was not James," she says while refilling both our glasses.

"No, that was James' cousin David. I don't know him very well, but he seems nice. I just invited him to come, I mean...I figure the more, the merrier," I shrug. "I'm not even sure he knows where we live, but he sounded as if he would figure it out."

"Well, I'm sure James will love it. Speaking of which..." Dez points outside the front window and indicates the car pulling into the drive. "I'd better go. You two have some making up to do." She smiles shyly and then shrugs on her coat, hugging me goodbye just as James enters the house.

"Hey, Dez, don't leave on my account," James says as he walks in, planting a kiss on her cheek in the hall.

"I was just leaving anyway. My job here is done!" She smiles at James and then reaches out to touch my arm. "I'll see you on Monday. Call if you need me."

She leaves, and we stand silently in the hallway for a moment.

"I'm sorry," we say it at the exact same moment.

We laugh, then look at each other.

"You first."

I say this to him, but then begin to speak anyway, as James puts a shushing finger to my lips.

"I'm sorry. I had a totally crap week at work, and I really

needed some serious time to veg. I'm sorry I forgot about the lights; I know how important all this is to you."

"I would like to think it's important to *us*."

James inclines his head, not quite a nod, then gives me a quick kiss on the lips.

"I just hate seeing you knocking yourself out for a bunch of people who could probably care less."

He says this, not realizing the impact, as I back away with a horrified look on my face.

"I thought we were calling a truce."

"We are. I'm sorry, I love you. Now what can I help with?"

And right there I chose to let it go. I grabbed his hand and ushered him into the kitchen, indicating the cookies that still needed to be packed into tins.

James reaches for a glittery menorah, inspects it, and shoves the entire cookie in his mouth.

Then he takes a swig from my wine.

"James! Those are for Hanukkah!" I admonish him as I decide to finish the glass Dez left behind.

"That one was for me right now. Yum."

"Did you eat?"

"Uncle Ben and I munched on some cheese and crackers and whatnot. Don't worry about me." He waves his hand away to indicate that food is unimportant, as he manages to shove another cookie down his throat.

He has his back turned and thinks I don't see him.

"Well, I test-ran a pasta recipe tonight, and I sure could use another opinion," I say, knowing that was all the invitation he needed.

"I can give one."

"You're sure you're up to it?"

"That I am."

"Good!" I flash him an easy smile as I lift a container into the microwave and begin to heat the leftover pasta.

Chapter Twenty-One

The ground must be frozen, because I can't remember these things being that hard to put in.

Of course, it would help if I was wearing something besides my flannel pajamas.

I grab the rounded top of the candy cane stake with all my might and try desperately to pull it out of the ground. On my next tug, I dig in, tug harder, and still manage to fall backward on my behind.

"OOOMMPH!" I say this a bit loud, considering the pre-dawn hour, and the sounds suddenly emanating from inside the house. As I get up and dust myself off, I see the lights going on, one by one, and then James standing at the door in his flannel pajamas.

"Sorry I woke you!" I give a wave as if to say there's nothing to see here. And really there's just me, with an open parka, hair askew, and boots thrown on quickly over pajama bottoms.

He looks bewildered.

I stand up straight and dust a thin layer of snow off my hands.

"Rhonda! I heard a loud noise and...what the hell are you doing out here, before the crack of dawn?!" He's coming out onto the lawn now, looking quite the mess himself.

"I was trying to begin the transformation without waking you up," I say a bit sheepishly, feeling caught in the act.

"The transformation?" He wipes the sleep out of his eyes and looks at me as if I am an alien creature. He crosses his arms across his chest, shivering, but still manages to give me a look.

The Look.

"Well, sure! I mean, Christmas is over...and I thought it would be nice to make the decorations more Hanukkah-friendly...or, at least...holiday-neutral." I shrug.

"And you're serious?"

I simply stare at him in response.

"Okay, let me get a real coat, and some shoes, and I'll come out and help you." He walks away grumbling and I let loose a wicked smile, as I begin collecting the reindeer off the lawn.

A few minutes later, he's helping me pull up candy cane stakes, stash the reindeer, and take all semblance of Christmas off the front lawn. We leave the Hanukkah lawn ornaments, plain white lights, a Frosty the Snowman figure, and a few snowflakes.

Once we're inside, I take a good look at my Christmas tree, then suddenly decide to pull off all the gold garland and replace it with silver. James insists I don't need to do this, but I soon have him on a ladder, and I'm issuing orders as he takes all the red and green balls off the tree and replaces them with blue.

From there, I survey the rest of the room. I stand in front of my fireplace, and it only takes a second to know what needs to be done.

I reach for the J-O-Y letters and begin to toss them aside, but stop as another idea hits me. I remove just the J, placing it on top of a box that James is carrying as he passes me by, and leave the 'OY!' up on the mantle.

Then, I waltz over to our CD player, pop out Neil Diamond's *A Cherry Cherry Christmas* and put in the soundtrack to *Fiddler on the Roof.*

Perfect.

Chapter Twenty-Two

"Is there anything else I can do for you?" James enters the kitchen just as I shut the oven.

I twirl around and adjust the tie on my Hanukkah apron, then indicate the various platters and wineglasses laid out all over the counters.

"Yes, sweetie, can you put those wineglasses out on the table?" I move towards my list.

"I think..." James begins to say something as I am crossing off list items. Just then, the doorbell rings, and as we look at each other, I let out a sound.

"...it's Showtime!"

"Okay, I'll start the latkes!" I pour the extremely lumpy batter onto a sizzling pan full of oil. I adjust the heat, and then go out to join James in welcoming his family.

"Happy Hanukkah, everybody!" I exclaim, air-kissing Vivian and Vlad as James takes their coats. Aunt Bunny shakes off her coat and gives me a big kiss, while Uncle Ben waits his turn and

Debby Caruso

then envelops me in a bear hug.

"Hey! How's my little Hanukkah Latke? And what happened to all the pretty Christmas decorations you had out last week?" He makes a sweeping gesture as if to take in the whole front yard, while handing James his coat, and me his hat.

"Well...I thought it would be nicer for all of you if we transformed the decorations! Strictly Hanukkah!"

I say this with vive.

"Like we care." This from Vivian. Not even a stage whisper.

"Of course we care that Rhonda went to all this trouble! Right, Viv?" He shoots her a warning look and Vivian rolls her eyes.

"Well, why don't you all come in and have a drink while we wait for Ira and Jill?" James ushers them from the hallway.

"Ugh, you gave in to the Jewish guilt and invited Ira?" Aunt Bunny elbows Uncle Ben and he laughs uproariously.

"Well, Rhonda did." James says as I shrug my shoulders.

"I think I just wanted it to be a nice big family Christ------- ah,Hanukkah. I also told your cousin David to stop by; he called and said he's going to be in the area."

"You never told me that," James insists.

"Sure I did." Of course I did.

"No, you didn't."

"I thought I did." I'm glaring at him now, willing him to give in, as the relatives converge on the assembled appetizers, pretending not to hear.

"Does David still think everyone is a criminal?" Uncle Ben inquires.

"Of course he does. He's the type of guy who never seems to know how to turn it off," James sighs.

84

"Oh, he's harmless, you two. And he's probably right. Just about everyone is a criminal nowadays. I think it's nice that Dave is coming; the more the merrier, that's what I always say!" Aunt Bunny chimes in.

"I agree. Thanks, Aunt Bunny, I'm sure he'll be fine, perhaps restrain himself because of the holiday." I shoot James a look just as the doorbell rings. In the next instant, Vivian wrinkles her nose and looks over towards me.

"Something's burning," she says blankly.

"OH! The latkes!" In an effort to save the latkes, I sprint from the living area into the kitchen, only to see the pan with the latkes spewing smoke into the air.

I quickly grab a potholder and pull the pan off the burner. The fire alarm begins a making a loud, harsh noise. Dez runs into the kitchen at that point, trying to scream over the horrible sound.

"What do we do?!" Dez yells.

"Tell James to shut it off and try and help me open up some windows." As we begin frantically opening up the windows, the alarm is finally silenced. James comes barreling into the kitchen a second later.

"What happened?"

"UGH! Well, I ruined the first batch of latkes… that's what happened." I'm on the verge of tears.

"You okay?"

"I'm fine. I just…" I push him away as he tries to comfort me. "Please. Just go tend to our guests."

James nods his head and looks over to Dez for help. They share a knowing look (which I catch) and Dez jumps in the minute James exits.

"What can I do to help you?" Dez takes the reins and I'm instantly grateful.

"I need to start again," I sigh.

"You couldn't make these in advance?"

"You can't make latkes in advance."

"Okay, so, what do you need me to do?" Dez is beginning to pace.

"I need you to go out there and be with your man. He is here, isn't he?" I try to move her towards the living area.

"He's a grown man who can chitchat on his own. Let me help you now." Dez is resolute.

"Okay." We begin the process of throwing out the first round, and then frying up new latkes. A few minutes later, the doorbell rings again and we hear the whole crowd say, "DAVID!" and, "So nice to see you!"

"Who's David?" Dez asks.

"James' cousin, who is a policeman, apparently 24/7." I shake my head.

"I betcha he's got some great stories."

"Yes. Well…"

The doorbell rings again, and we exchange a look as we begin piling latkes high on a plate.

"Hail, hail, the gang's all here."

We finish the task at hand and then make our way out to the crowd. Assembled around the dining room table are James, Vivian and Vlad, Uncle Ben and Aunt Bunny, Grandma, Cousins Ira, Jill, and David, as well as Jack, Dez's flame.

"Even Frosty the Snowman is a perp! We should call him Frosty the Snow--Perp or…Frosty the Perp-Man!" David expostulates.

"How do you figure?" Ira looks at David as if he is simply out of his gourd.

"He's saying, 'Catch me if you can!' Remember what he did to the traffic cop?! He only paused a MOMENT when he heard him holler, 'STOP!' David is nodding his head as if to say, "SEE?!"

"Don't you think that's a bit much, Dave?" Ira exhales loudly.

"Well, he was disobeying a direct order. When a cop tells you to stop, YOU STOP!" This is punctuated with hand signals and full-out agitation. I'm getting nervous that David will spontaneously combust and ruin the table setting.

Uncle Ben shakes his head and looks at James indicating, *who invited this nutjob?* James shakes his head and shrugs. At the same moment, Dez begins laughing and Jack follows suit.

"Well, Dave, I'm sure you have a lot of exciting stories. My job is pretty mundane. The most exciting thing to ever happen to me on a ladder was meeting Desiree," Jack interjects, and the ladies at the table all give an *aww* sound while the guys roll their eyes in unison.

"I'm a lucky girl!" Dez elbows him as she makes this announcement, then turns to Jill. "Jill, can you please pass the latkes?"

"Sure," Jill says in a barely audible voice, then picks up a nearby platter with one hand, almost tips it, but manages to right it quickly. She passes it silently over to Dez.

"So what's up, Jilly-Bean? I haven't heard a peep out of you yet today! You have any new news to share with the group?" Uncle Ben has a twinkle in his eye as he says this, and all heads turn towards Jill.

Jill turns to Ira and whacks him in the arm—hard. Then she bursts into tears, leaving the entire family stunned and staring.

I am about to crawl under the table and never come out.

"You...told...them?!" Now she's glaring at Ira, her lower lip quivering, ice in her eyes. Everybody else is deadly silent.

"Jill, I haven't told anybody anything. I think Uncle Ben means..." Ira tries but she cuts him off hard.

"You had NO right!" She reaches for Ira's wineglass and downs the entire glass of wine in one gulp.

"Jill, you really shouldn't..." He gives her a warning glance, and his eyes flit ever-so-quickly around the table.

"Why? Like it matters now!" Jill bangs down the wine-glass, stands up, places her hands firmly on her hips, and then announces through tears; "I just had a miscarriage. That's the 'NEW NEWS' for all of you!"

With that, she scrapes back her chair and runs from the room, hysterically crying. We hear her stumble into the bathroom and slam the door shut behind her.

There is total silence at the table. Ira is looking down at his plate, and everyone else is sitting still, shocked by this sudden announcement.

I am definitely going to crawl under the table, and perhaps stay there until New Year's Eve.

"Ira, I am so sorry...I meant...your Aunt Bunny told me she got some sort of work promotion..." Uncle Ben is at a loss for words.

"Should I go after her?" I offer this as the day slips right through my fingers, my enchanted holiday all but ruined.

"Rhonda, you're not a mother. You can't possibly understand what it's like to lose a child. I'll go," Vivian says in her imperial fashion as she gets up to leave the table.

In an effort to salvage any part of the day, I stand and announce that I'm going to get the lasagne. I'm choking back tears, but I can still offer them food.

"Latkes and lasagne! That's my kind of meal!" Grandma puts this in and everyone laughs just a little too hard.

"Anything is better than the fast food I get stuck eating all the time. I can recite the Dollar Menu for you, alphabetically, off the top of my head!" David does a strange eye roll/shake the head combo at this point.

"Which Dollar Menu?" Jack asks, and I see Dez elbow him.

"Any of 'em! You want Mickey D's, Popeyes, which one?" David offers this up as a challenge.

"Oh, I love that Popeye chicken. Ben, when's the last time we had any of that?" Aunt Bunny, God love her.

I make a clean escape and manage to hold back the actual tears until I reach the relative safety of my kitchen. I'm about to grab the lasagne, but gravitate towards the window instead, where I stare straight ahead at nothing. A moment later I feel James come up behind me and wrap his arms around me, settling his chin on my shoulder.

"Hey, sweetie, really, it's fine. It's all good out there. Please don't pay any attention to the Holiday Edition of Crazy at the Golden's."

"I just don't understand why your mother has to act that way," I sniffle.

James lifts his chin and turns me towards him.

"What way?"

"*You can't possibly understand what it's like to lose a child...*" I have to say, my Vivian imitation is spot-on.

"Well, you can't. Don't take it personally."

He's so matter-of-fact I want to scream.

"Since it's directed towards me, how else am I supposed to take it?" I counter.

"Please, Rhonda, don't let her bother you. She's...that's just the way she is, and she's not about to change." Now it's his turn to sigh.

"Well, she can try being a little bit nicer to me." A bell chimes and I make a run for the oven, determined not to burn the lasagne at this point too. I carefully lift the tray out of the oven, placing it on top of the stove.

"And you can try lowering your expectations."

"What's that supposed to mean?"

"It means exactly what I just said." With that, James grabs the salad off the counter and exits the kitchen.

I go to grab the tray of lasagne without my oven mitts and almost burn myself.

"Ouch!" I dash over to the sink and run my finger under ice cold water for a second.

After that, I take a deep breath and exit the kitchen, back into the lion's den.

Chapter Twenty-Three

The detritus of dessert all around the table, one by one the assembled guests begin to make advances towards leaving.

Jill's seat is still empty.

"I think I'm going try and pry Jill out of the bathroom now," Ira announces as he pushes away from the table.

"Ira, you take her home and make her a nice, hot cup of tea. And let her eat chocolate, or drink wine...whatever the hell she wants. She's in mourning. It's your responsibility to take care of her right now." Vivian barks orders at him, the same way she does to everyone else, completely unaware of how she sounds.

It occurs to me that she doesn't care.

"I know, Aunt Viv. Thanks so much to all of you...it's been... very hard on Jill. On both of us, actually." With that, Ira exits the dining area and goes to collect Jill.

"I'll pack up some Hanukkah cookies for Jill." I make my way back into the relative safety of the kitchen with Dez carrying a half-empty tray of cookies.

"Let me help you, girl." She pulls a Hanukkah tin from a nearby shelf and begins to fill it with cookies for Jill.

I nod my head as the tears start to flow, and not a second later I feel Dez offer me a hug. She crushes me, and I basically hang on for dear life.

"It's just...I wanted a day where everything turned out so perfect. And I really and truly feel like nothing did." I am defeated. I continue to cry softly into Dez's shirt.

"Rhonda, you are way too hard on yourself, girl, now stop it." She pushes me away from her and forces me to look her in the eye. "You did a far better job than I could ever do...after Jill left, everyone settled in and enjoyed the lasagne and the company. You cannot control Jill; she's clearly fixated on having a baby and there's very little anyone can do to help her. That has *nothing* to do with you."

"Oh, believe me, I know that. I get it; I even feel incredibly sorry for her. But then how come Vivian can help her?" I make a frustrated sound.

"Vivian just thinks she can help her, and Vlad is a smart enough guy to let her think it. He was probably thrilled that she spent a couple of hours in the bathroom with Jill!"

I start to laugh and Desiree follows suit.

"Don't think I don't mean it." Dez closes the tin and smiles wickedly. "Come on, let's bid them all adieu."

By the time we exit the kitchen, we find everyone getting up from the table, gathering purses and coats and all manner of things, making their way towards the door. I follow them out, handing each a fistful of gelt and thanking them for coming.

"Remember, Hanukkah lasts all week! Feel free to drop in if

you want to light another candle!" I say it gaily, although I don't feel that way, but I try anyway.

Dez is the last to leave, and I give her yet another hug, then wave to both her and Jack as the car pulls out of the driveway. Once everyone is gone, James closes the door, leans against it, and looks at me. He lets out a huge sigh of relief, and then a loud "WHEW!"

"Please tell me we are never going to attempt to pull that off again!" He chuckles, mostly to himself, and follows me back into the kitchen.

"Was it that bad?" I'm cringing, waiting for his response.

"You know what, Rhon? It was exactly what I thought it would be. Barring Jill's hysterics, that is..."

He throws his hands in the air, as if helpless to say any more.

"Well, I just think Jill really wants a baby." I have about nothing left to say either.

"You think?" James pulls a face.

"Yeah, I kind of caught that." I begin busying myself with the putting away of things, as James pours the last of a bottle of wine into a glass and settles on a kitchen stool.

"Can I help with anything?" he offers.

"Yeah. Yes. You can help with your attitude. I was hoping you would act a little bit more...on my side here, James." I'm being pissy and I know it, but feel unable to stop right now.

"How have I not been on your side?!" He seems completely taken aback and even sets the wine glass down.

"Really? You can't figure it out? Well, why don't we start with how you totally took your mother's side after she so rudely informed me that I was not equipped to help soothe Jill?!" I shove a dish into the dishwasher as punctuation.

"I didn't take her side! I just said that maybe you can't under-stand...wait a minute, what's this all about here? Your perfect day was slightly less than perfect, so now you've decided to take it out on me? I'm the one who should be a little teed off here! You invited my cousin David and never even told me! David is a total idiot, as evidenced by his 'Frosty-the-Snowman-is-a-Big -Fat-Burglar' speech!"

"He's a Perp," I correct him.

"A what?"

"It's short for perpetrator. It doesn't matter. It's just..." Now I throw the dishtowel down on the island.

"It's just what?"

"It's just that, all my life, my mother and I would knock ourselves out to create...the perfect holiday...beautiful memo-ries...whatever you want to call it, and every year, every time, my father would be so disaffected by all of it...like whatever happened was fine by him, like he couldn't care less, and..." I'm crying again, this time serious tears.

"Well, he probably couldn't care less. I mean..."

I'm losing it now. And James is just sitting there, completely inept.

"I didn't mean it to come out like that, Rhonda, I'm sorry."

I don't respond.

"I think I'm going to take a walk. I need a little air." He pushes his wine glass back on the counter and stalks out of the room.

A minute later I hear a door opening and closing.

Another minute and the doorbell rings.

"Oh, he probably turned around and realized...forgot his

keys…" I'm scraping at tears as I run towards the door, fully expecting to see James.

I open the door with an expectant smile only to find Uncle Ben standing on the other side.

"Oh, Uncle Ben! Hi!" I peer around him; no James.

"Well, help me Rhonda, but I think I left my hat behind!" He enters the foyer and stands there smiling.

"Oh! Of course. Let me just…" I pull the hall closet open and locate Uncle Ben's hat on the top shelf. I pass it over to him and offer what could only be classified as a weak smile.

"Ah, thanks. I think it's obligatory for an old man to wear a hat in winter." He chuckles, and then, in his Uncle Ben way, leans into me. "Where's James?"

"UGH!" I slam the closet door and clench my fists, about ready to cry again. "He just took off, he…" I can't even finish my sentence.

"Oh, no, kiddo, hey…hey…" Uncle Ben starts patting me on the back as he wraps me in a sturdy hug. I just cry.

"Let's go sit down. I want to talk to you a minute," Uncle Ben suggests.

I must have nodded, because I allow him to steer me into the living room, where we settle on a couch beside the dying fire.

"I know you're upset kiddo, but you really don't need to be. You did a fine job today. You made us all a fabulous Hanukkah, one of the best celebrations I've had in years."

"Yeah right. Did you like the burned latkes or the Jill Meltdown best?" I'm pouting at this point so I stare into the burning embers of the fire and cross my arms, planting them firmly across my chest.

"The lasagne was delicious," Uncle Ben says.

"Uncle Ben, can I ask you something without you getting offended or taking sides?"

"Of course you can."

"Why is Vivian so hostile towards me?" I reposition myself on the couch then and look directly at Uncle Ben.

"Well..." He looks uncomfortable for a moment, and then I see a decision being made, and a second later he takes a deep breath and dives in. "Let me start by asking you this: what has James ever told you about his real father?"

I regard him quizzically, obviously thrown off guard by the question.

"His real father?"

"Yes. Not Vlad. James' real father's name was Curtis."

"I never even knew his name. Well, he's told me very little, basically because I don't think he remembers a lot. Why?" Now my interest is piqued, and I'm not exactly sure where this whole thing is going.

"Well, you have to remember things were very different back when you and James were little. Divorce was not as common, and visitation with said children of divorce was sort of fast and loose; rarely did the courts get involved in custody issues the way they do today."

"Okay..."

"So! Vivian and Curtis were a nightmare. They were doomed from the get-go. They had a volatile relationship and truthfully, I think the only good thing to come out of it was James. Their divorce wasn't easy, and Curtis was always a shady character. One weekend when he was supposed to have James for visitation, he kept him."

"Kept him? What do you mean, '*kept him?*'"

"I mean just that. I think he was supposed to return him on a Sunday, and he never did. At first, we weren't too alarmed; Curtis was always late. Vivian tried frantically to call him, and he never answered. Keep in mind we didn't have cell phones back then."

He took a deep breath and continued.

"Eventually, I took Viv over to his apartment to try and pick James up, but they weren't there. We ran around and went to all his usual haunts...no James, no Curtis. Your Aunt Bunny sat over at Vivian's waiting for a call that never came. We called David's father who was also a policeman..." Uncle Ben pauses a second to make a face: like father, like son...*NUTS*... "and there was nothing they could do right away. It was a custody thing, they said, and they assured Vivian that he would return the kid eventually."

"Oh my God. Today, they would have put out an Amber Alert, and gotten the dogs ready..." My mind was officially blown.

"You betcha. But that was then, and Vivian was beside herself. She felt trapped by the phone, and yet she wanted to be out there, looking for her son. She was desperate, and hysterical. For almost two days there was nothing."

"And then?"

"And then David's father called. He had a lead. Apparently, Curtis's friend owned a cabin on a lake upstate. He grabbed his partner, I grabbed Viv, and we made our way up there on nothing more than a hunch, and a really bad map."

"And you found him there?"

"We did. Thankfully, James didn't really know what was going on. Curtis had told him they were going on a little vacation, and

James loved his Dad, so he never thought to question him. I'll never forget the look on Vivian's face, the moment that kid ran back into her arms."

"Is that why James has no relationship with his father?"

"Basically, I think Vivian told him that if he stuckaround, he'd be up for kidnapping charges. Oh, he made some noise after that, but he knew he was in the wrong, and he knew Vivian would never let him have the kid again."

"So she's overprotective?"

"To put it mildly. She...is terrified of losing him. She always was a panic, but that weekend changed her for good. She will forever think that she's the only one who knows what's best for him. Afterward, she often said she would give anything to rewind, and take back that weekend...to do it all over again...be more perceptive, whatever-she's stuck, and that's why she says the things she says. Even though I think deep down she likes you, she just doesn't seem to know any other way."

"I guess that makes more sense than anything else I've tried to figure. I can't imagine...you know, she was right today. I can't imagine what it's like to lose a child." Now I didn't know how to feel. This revelation certainly changed the way I saw Vivian.

"She could still do a little better with you; believe me, her hostility doesn't go unnoticed by me, or Aunt Bunny, or even James."

"I think James just doesn't see it."

"He does, he just doesn't always know how to deal with her. He loves you both, and I think he wants peace at all costs. All Viv wants is a rewind button...and all James wants is some peace."

"I think we all want a rewind button sometimes."

"You'd think with all the recycling going on nowadays...you think they'd find a way to recycle scenes from your life!" Uncle Ben chuckles and pats me on the arm. I'm sitting still, but the moment he says this, I have a 'light bulb moment,' and I just about launch myself straight off the couch.

"UNCLE BEN! THAT'S IT!" I begin pointing at him and gesturing wildly.

"What's it?" He looks bewildered.

"You just said something...OH MY GOD...I've got to call Dez; thank you, Uncle Ben, thank you so much!" I lean over to give him a big smacker on the cheek and then I lunge towards my cell phone which is sitting on the nearby coffee table. I push Dez's number and when Dez answers, I shout, "Dez, I got it! WE GOT IT! Actually, Uncle Ben just got it for us!"

"What are you talking about?" Dez returns with a voice that says she already has her fuzzy slippers on.

"The campaign! You've got to meet me! Right now! Come here..."

"I just left there."

"I know! Okay, meet me at the office."

"NOW?!"

"Yes, NOW! NOW, NOW, NOW!! Grab your passkey and meet me now. I think I just wrapped up the whole *Splash* campaign!"

"This better be good, Rhon."

"I promise. It's the best!" I hang up the phone and do a little dance in the center of the room. By the time I look up, I see Uncle Ben staring at me as if I have just gone off the deep end.

"Uncle Ben, you're the best. But I've got to go! I've got to strike while the iron is hot! Oh, you can stay...I'm so sorry, but I've got to go meet Dez."

"No, no, that's fine. I really just stopped by to grab my hat. I'll follow you out."

"Thanks! You're the best!" I'm repeating myself but it's all I can say, as my mind is whirring with possibilities.

"Who knew I could be so helpful?" Uncle Ben says this we make our way out of the house, and as I pull out of the drive, Uncle Ben waves to me and shakes his head once again.

I love that man.

Chapter Twenty-Four

I march into the office, throw on the lights, and shrug off my coat. I grab a marker and make for the whiteboard, furiously scribbling, the thoughts tumbling out faster than I can put them down.

A few minutes later Dez breezes in with a hat askew, one glove on, and plaid pajama pants under a pea coat.

"I'm here."

"AH! You scared me!" Once I'm in my head...I'm in my head.

Dez rolls her eyes and tries to look beyond me to my various notes.

"Rhonda, I have a very hot guy semiconscious, waiting for me with baited breath in my apartment. This had better be good," Dez threatens as she takes off her outerwear.

"It is so good. Are you ready?" I step away from the whiteboard, arm extended, and point to where the words "RECYCLE YOUR LIFE" stand out in bold. Underneath the catch phrase are several boxes, filled with doodles of people doing various things, and some form of *Splash* beverage in the frame.

Desiree nods while taking it in, still peeling off the one glove.

"You know what Artie would say?" Dez finally asks.

"Look eye?"

"Sell it to me!"

"Okay! Here's the concept…" I pause a second while Dez settles into a nearby chair, rapt with attention.

"If you were to rewind---or, in this case, *recycle*---your life, wouldn't all the happiest scenes be shown with a *Splash* beverage in hand?" I point to the various frames. "That summer vacation that you thought would never end? The first time you got to go to the movies alone with your friends? That big Fourth of July BBQ that Uncle Jimmy always throws, with a barrel full of *Splash* beverages on ice nearby? How about the first time you take your new baby in a pool, a *Splash* beverage sitting right at the water's edge?"

"Can we use the tree that Ramon drew for the original concept?"

"Why not? We can have him draw snapshots, shooting off the branches, with the tag line, *Recycle Your Life!* Directly underneath it, we can say something to the effect of…I don't know yet…but something like… '*Splash. Only recycle the best scenes.'*" I am jumping out of my skin here, waiting for her to buy it.

"I like the tag line. In fact, I almost forgive you for ripping me out of my near slumber, not to mention

Jack's warm arms." Dez shoots me a look and begins to pace in front of the whiteboard, getting excited about the concept. "We can have a woman reminiscing about that first time at the movies without the parents, three giggling girls with *Splash* beverages in hand, then she picks up the phone and calls her friend now-older, of course; we'd need to use two actresses-and asks her if she wants to go to a movie. As she hangs up the phone, the camera zeroes in on a *Splash* beverage sitting next to her on the counter."

"YES! And we can use the old look, the retro-cans for the past scene, and the new bottles and logos in the scenes depicting today..." We're humming along now.

"We're selling nostalgia..." Dez points out.

"And we're using the whole green concept they wanted, by using the word recycle..."

"I think Artie will go for it." Dez is nodding and pacing now.

"Let's call the whole team!" I suggest.

"Rhonda! It is...right now, it is 1:30 in the morning. It is the day after Christmas. Absolutely nobody wants to deal with this until we get back. And why are you so eager to camp out here? Don't you have a nice, warm body to go home to, too?"

"Not so much." I fall into the chair opposite Dez and let out a huge sigh.

"What happened after I left?"

I'm clicking a retractable Sharpie, mulling my words.

"Ugh, I got into it with James."

"About what?" Dez is leveling her gaze at me now, so I scrunch up my face and let out another sigh before answering.

"About his mother. About the fact that he doesn't make as big of a deal about the holidays as I do...about David being Super-Cop...I don't know, Dez, it was about everything." I chuck the Sharpie.

"It sounds like it's about you."

"What are you talking about?"

"Rhon, I've known you how long?"

"Forever."

"Okay. So I think that qualifies me to say a few things here. First off, the entire Holiday Jubilee was totally up to you. You kept making it seem like you were doing it for James, but you were really doing it for you."

"Why would you say that?"

"Because I know. I know you. I love you, Rhon, but I think you are still trying to create that perfect holiday. Not to mention... re-create the worst one."

"What perfect holiday? The one I never had?!" My eyes begin to well up.

Desiree sighs audibly and lets me go on.

"Or the one when my mother died?" I'm keening in pain, doubled over now, and Desiree comes over and begins to stroke my back.

"You never talk about it, babe. I can't imagine how awful it was, but maybe you need to talk about it."

"I can't...even put into words how horrible it felt to wake up Christmas morning and find out that my mother had died. I remember getting up and barreling down to the tree...only to find my father sitting at the table, a mug in his hand, tears on his cheeks...that Christmas Eve...that last Christmas...I can't seem to get past it, and neither can he...I just wanted this holiday to erase some of the pain. Who knows? Maybe I wanted a little bit of mothering from Vivian, or on some level, I wanted to recycle my own life."

"That's okay. All of it, it's okay that you want to erase the bad memories and write new ones; fun ones, good ones. But you see, there is no perfect day; there is no perfect holiday. It's what you make of it."

"I can't stop thinking that maybe if I had different players in the game, so to speak, that I would have a better time...a different outcome."

"But you don't. For better or for worse, these are the people God gave you to travel through life with. Each year, you can line them all up, you can bake your ass off, hell, you can even haul in a whole buffer crew of ragtag individuals from the neighborhood...but in the end, you're always going to have the same players in the game."

"And therefore the same outcome."

"Maybe. Maybe not. The only one you can change is you. Think of it this way: the only one you even *chose* was James. And me, of course."

I smile at this.

"Of course!" I put my head in my hands.

"I hate this. I just want to have an idyllic holiday. Just once. I want the food to be perfect, and the jokes to be funny, I want to not have any drama, and I want everybody to leave my house with a warm fuzzy feeling inside. Is that too much to ask?"

"In the big scheme of things, it's probably not too much to ask. It's also not reality. Listen to me: remember how you wanted to choke the wedding singer by the end of the night at your wedding?"

"Remember? I still have fantasies about shoving the microphone down her throat!" I laugh out loud as I picture it.

"Okay, that's fine. So long as it all stays in your head. My point is, you were upset because she mispronounced everyone's name and kept saying stupid things into the microphone."

"She was drunk, Dez, and a huge hot mess," I feel the need to clarify.

"I agree. But I know you very well, so I know that about you, therefore I know that you will ruminate over this Blondie-Wannabe from now until the end of time."

"So?"

"So, do you think anyone else even remembers what she looked like?"

"Your point is?"

"My point is, how do you know that everyone didn't leave your home with a warm, fuzzy feeling tonight? Just because it wasn't perfect for you, doesn't mean it wasn't great for everyone else."

"Uncle Ben did say the word fabulous and Hanukkah in the same sentence."

"Exactly! I love Uncle Ben; he makes my life so much easier. Look, it's way past two. Why don't you go home and sleep on it, and we'll deal with the campaign and anything else you want to talk about tomorrow?"

"I can do that."

"I'm here for you, always. You know that, don't you?"

"Of course I do. Now go!" I make a shooing motion and offer out an uneven smile.

"Thank God. I'm tired, and I need to curl up next to my new man." Dez grabs her stuff and urges me to do the same. "It will all still be here tomorrow."

Chapter Twenty-Five

I awaken to the sunlight filtering in through the blinds. I blink, take a deep breath, and roll over to face James' back.

He is silent.

I crawl towards him and wrap my arm around him from behind. There is no movement.

I decide to go for it and lunge over him, putting my face right up in his.

"Hey, are you still sleeping?" Annoying, sure. But it works.

"I was trying to...what time is it?" he grumbles.

"I don't know, I just woke up myself." I try a smile.

"What time did you get in last night?" he asks sleepily.

"Late. I met..."

He totally cuts me off as he suddenly sits up and gives me a long look.

"You never even left me a note, or called to tell me where you were going," he accuses.

"I'm sorry, I had a...'

"Were you that upset, Rhonda? Because I really can't pretend to be invested in this holiday thing any more than I already am...I mean, I tried like hell to remember to light the tree, and help you out. I tasted all your cookies and, I mean, I tried, I really did, but I'm afraid it's just not good enough for you and it never will be. I'm sorry."

"Oh, James, that's the thing. It is good enough. I'm sorry I compared you to my father."

"Well, I'm sorry I said he could care less. I don't really know how he feels; I just know that you take all of this so personally, and I don't know what else I can do. I know you miss your Mom and…"

I cut him off now. "I do, I miss her and the holidays are just not the same without her. Listen," I take a deep breath and strike a solemn pose, "I had a long talk with Uncle Ben last night and-"

"Uncle Ben? I thought he left before I did."

"He did. Then he came back because he forgot his hat, and we talked. He told me about what happened with your father."

"Vlad? What happened with Vlad?"

"James, your real father."

"Oh."

"James, how come you never told me about that whole thing, the lake house...your Mom? It explains so much."

"I just don't like to think about it."

"Do you ever think about him?"

"Curtis? Not really...I can barely remember what he looks like. I only know that he scared my mother, and for that alone I don't want to know him."

"I understand. I hope you're not mad at Uncle Ben for sharing your story with me; I think he told me in an effort to have me better understand Vivian."

"Look, I know my mother's not easy. Don't think for one minute it escapes me...she can be a real pain in the ass, even when she's not trying. But I don't know how else to deal with her. I wish my grandfather was still alive...he always knew how to get her to tone it down...or I wish maybe we had known each other a little longer before we got married. Maybe if she had a little more time to adjust to the idea of you..." He trails off here so I step back in.

"I don't know if that would have helped. What I do know is that she's still holding on to her fear of losing you, and it crops up in a million little different ways, and sometimes...well, sometimes she can be a little tough."

"A little? I think she won the gold medal for Acid Tongue in the last three Olympics."

We share a laugh and then I settle into the crook of his arm.

He kisses my forehead and says; "What exactly are we going to do with each other?"

"I have a few ideas..."

Chapter Twenty-Six

I'm tapping yet another Sharpie furiously, while the entire *Team Splash* is settled around me in the conference room, each person shouting to be heard over the next. Well, the word *settled* is a bit much, as the room keeps getting louder, and everyone sounds vaguely unhinged.

I shoot Dez a look.

"OKAY! Let's reign it all in, people! We've got Artie calling in about..." Dez checks her watch theatrically, "one hour. And unless we want to work every single second of our week between Christmas and New Year's...let's decide how we're going to present it to him, and therefore the client."

There's much buzzing around the room, the discussing of art and theme, while barbs are being traded and snacks are being consumed.

Once the clock strikes two, I stand up and gather the group together.

"Okay, guys, it's time to call Artie! Just remember...we have a great campaign! Let's sell it to him!"

There is a smattering of applause.

Then we all wait silently while I dial Artie's phone from the conference table phone that resembles a spaceship. The phone rings four times and then Artie appears on the video screen at the front of the conference room. He is wearing what looks like a Hugh-Hefner style smoking jacket, mimosa in hand, a bottle of aspirin in the foreground. In the background, we see a good-looking man brushing his teeth with only his underwear on.

"Hello, my Pretties! Are we all assembled?"

I'm trying not to laugh.

"Yes, hi Artie, it's *Team Splash*, and we think we've got the new campaign ready to roll."

"Sell it to me!" Artie barks.

The toothbrushing man disappears from the background and we hear a toilet flush. There's a ton of commotion on screen as I begin my pitch, and then we all pause as Artie looks over his shoulder in bewilderment.

"Can you hold on a sec?" Artie gets up from his perch and barrels toward the bathroom, throwing open the door, only to find his lover entwined in a shower curtain on the floor.

"I fell," Artie's man states the obvious as the entire conference room is just about dying.

"Are you okay? You look...ridiculous! And can you puh-leese be quiet in here? I'm on a conference call!"

Artie slams the door behind him and stalks back towards the camera, his smoking jacket trailing behind him with each step.

The team stifles a collective giggle.

"Okay! Are we ready? Sell it to me!" He's in control again so I begin my pitch, with Dez throwing in her ideas, as the whole team begins detailing the prospective artwork that can go into print, radio, television, and internet advertising. After a couple of intense minutes, I sit back down and let out a sigh.

"So? What do you think?" The room is silent, each team member waiting with baited breath to hear Artie's response.

"Is that everything?" Artie asks.

Dez and I share a nervous look.

"Yes, well, we can expand on the theme by-" I try, but he cuts me off completely before I even finish my sentence.

"I LOVE IT! I love it, *Splash* is going to fall in love with it, and we may very well have another CLIO award on our hands here! Good work, Team! I knew you could do this...and now, I can ski! Enjoy the rest of the week and we will expound upon this as soon as I get back!" Artie clicks himself off the call and there is an eruption in the room as an exhausted bunch of creatives congratulates one another. Dez and I whoop it up and bear hug.

"You happy now?"

"I'm getting there. I'll catch up with you later." I head out of the building and dial James.

I'm humming to myself as I exit the agency, thinking about the way the whole thing went down. James picks up on the second ring.

"Hey! Where are you?" I'm smiling wide, I can feel it in the cold, and I wonder if my cheeks will stick that way.

"I'm home. Why, where are you?"

"Walking over to the wine store to buy Uncle Ben a bottle of his favorite wine. By the way, what is Uncle Ben's favorite wine?"

I decide he totally deserves it.

"It's called Any. Any wine. So tell me, did Artie like it?"

I simply let out a loud whooping sound.

"He actually said the word LOVE! And he thinks that *Splash* will love it too! Oh, I can't wait to tell Uncle Ben the whole story! I'll call you when I'm on my way home."

"Okay, see you soon."

"Love you."

"Love you. Bye."

We hang up as I wind my way through a maze of boxes and wine bottles stuck into rack upon rack. Just as I'm pulling a bottle out to take a look, I hear a voice behind me say, "That's a cheap wine that doesn't taste cheap. A good choice, if you ask me."

I whirl around to find my father grinning at me.

"Hey Dad! Fancy meeting you here!"

"I was just about to say the same thing. So who's the lucky recipient?" He nods towards the wine.

"Oh! Uncle Ben. He...helped me out a lot on Hanukkah."

"So how was the shindig?"

I bristle but pretend to be reading the label.

"It went well. You should have come."

He ignores my second comment and says, "Well, good. So do you have time to grab a bite with Dear Old Dad?" He looks at me expectantly, as I grab two bottles of the same wine. We make our way towards the counter to pay.

"How about coffee, Dad? I have enough time for a cup of cappuccino...if you're buying, that is."

"What kind of guy invites a girl out but doesn't pick up the check?" He winks at me as the man behind the counter bags our purchases. A moment later we're exiting the store and making our way across the street to a small cafe called *The Holy Roast*.

My father indicates the sign as he pulls open the door.

"Either the guy's got a sense of humor or he's a religious fanatic."

"I vote for religious fanatic."

"'Tis the season."

We order drinks and then settle into a quiet corner with the steaming brew. I involve myself with all manner of sugar and stirrers, then push them away and confront my father head-on.

"Dad, can we talk?"

"Of course. What's on your mind?"

I take a deep breath and settle my cup.

"You've been awfully Grinchy." He tries to interject, but I hold up my palm in an effort to stop any interruptions. I scrunch up my nose, trying to put a smiley face on my remark, even as I wait a few beats.

He jumps in anyway.

"I just don't like the holidays anymore; your mother took all the joy with her when she left. Don't get me wrong, I don't hate them either. I just don't care."

"Well, can we change that?"

"What are you, Dr. Philistine?"

I roll my eyes at his nickname for Dr. Phil.

"I don't know, Doc, I think I have a hard time seeing the point in all of it...the hoopla...the rush...the amount of crazy people get...Rhonda, what are you asking me?" He seems uncomfortable, but I'm not willing to call this train back to the station.

Merry Hanukkah

"I was just wondering why you seem so uptight and disinterested this time of the year...if it all has to with Mom, or if you are simply not into it. We never talk about it. You know, the majority of the people in the world are full of peace and joy, you know, good will towards men. That sort of thing."

"Rhonda, let's not talk about the people in this world." He wraps air quotes around the *'people in this world.'* "If you have something to say, just say it." Then he levels his expression on mine and seems amazed when one thin tear begins its descent down my cheek.

"Well. I know you might not be able to understand this, but it hurts."

"What hurts?"

"It...hurts...me...when you act as if you could care less about the holidays...be it Christmas, or Hanukkah, or whatever...it hurts when you put so much emotion and work and passion into something, and one of the people you love the most can't even see or acknowledge all your effort. Can you understand how that would bother me?"

Dad begins slowly nodding.

"But Miss Golden, I never knew this bothered you so much." He splays his hands on the table.

"It does. I know it's not the same without her...it never will be...but I want to try and make it better, because at one time, we used to really have a good time."

"You're right."

"We did, right? And I really thought I had learned to live with it. I figured that the holidays would never be the same-and they could never be the same-but maybe they should still

115

be something we can share. I've ignored your sadness, and your silly jabs and offhand comments for years, thinking that it didn't bother me too much... not enough to mention it, that is...but I've decided that I need to tell you, because I need you to know."

"Well, I'm sorry Rhonda. Really and truly sorry. What can I do to make it up to you?"

"Can't you just fake it?" We both laugh, easing the tension, and my Dad nods his head to acquiesce.

"I can try, but no promises on that end."

"Well, I do have one idea," and my mind starts whirring again.

Chapter Twenty-Seven

I enter the house with two wine bottles in one hand and a bag of groceries in the other. I call out for James.

"Honey! I'm home!"

"In here."

I enter the living area to find James with Chinese takeout all laid out on the coffee table. There are candles lit and a bottle of wine chilling in a bucket filled with ice.

"Oh, how nice! I bought wine too..." I run to place my packages on the kitchen counter and return to the living area, taking it all in with a wide smile on my face.

"Well, I figured you've done enough cooking lately. And since this is what most Jewish people eat on Christmas Eve, well...I figured we were still keeping with the holiday tradition."

I take him in and smile at him.

"I'm so sorry; I think I tried to turn Hanukkah into Christmas."

"You think? No, Rhonda, what would make you think that?

Could it be that my Christmas tree-my first one ever-was magically transformed into a Hanukkah Bush the day after Christmas? Or that I actually have Hanukkah inflatables on my front lawn? I mean, I've been Jewish my whole life and I never even knew they made those things." He's making fun of me, but I'm allowing it because...well, the Chinese food smells good.

I put my hands up in a defensive posture, then begin laughing along with him.

"Did I screw up that royally?"

"Sweetie, your heart was in the right place, and that's all that matters." He ushers me to sit down and pours us each a glass of wine.

"It's sad actually...the whole reason I always liked Hanukkah growing up was because it was the untouched holiday...it seemed so much more important than Christmas, holier somehow...I can remember going over to my friend Ruthie's house when I was a kid, and standing there in awe, taking it all in, the candles, the tradition..." I trail off, then look pointedly at James. "I have an idea to fix it, though."

"Oh no. If it has anything to do with additional exterior illumination, I'm out of it." He waves me away with a chopstick.

"No, it doesn't. You're just going to have to try to trust me."

"I do trust you. It's Holiday Rhonda I don't trust. Now have some Moo Shu Pork and let's discuss." He taps the carton.

"What kind of Jew orders Moo Shu Pork on the second night of Hanukkah?"

"The same kind that has Frosty the Snow Perp on his front lawn."

We laugh and dig in.

Chapter Twenty-Eight

In order for this whole thing to work, I know what I have to do. So although I am walking up the path to their house with purpose, I find myself fidgeting nonetheless. At the door, I adjust the flowers, my purse and cell before lifting the handle on a brass knocker, planted firmly in the center of the door.

I wait a minute, then hear a voice call from inside.

I'm letting out a Pilates breath as Vlad swings open the door.

"Rhonda! Rhonda! To what do I owe this pleasure?"

"Hi, Vlad." I give him an awkward hug and sneak a peek behind him as he lets me into the entry.

"I was hoping...is Vivian around?"

"Ah, yes, she just got back from getting the nails done." He makes a gesture as if surveying his own nails, then blows on them, for emphasis. He laughs.

"I'll get her. Come, sit." He ushers me into the sitting room, and I take my coat off and begin to sit, not quite sure where to place the flowers. I eventually place the flowers gently on top of my coat and cross the room to look at a picture of James and his grandfather atop the fireplace mantle. They both have on baseball caps and are grinning widely for the camera.

"Any day that had baseball in it was a good day."

I swing around to find Vivian at the other end of the room, watching me take in the photograph. I smile hopefully.

"I think James still uses that expression."

Vivian raises an eyebrow and begins to cross the room. She walks over to a sideboard and starts clinking ice into a glass, her back turned to me.

"Would you like a drink?"

It's all very soap-opera-like and feels a bit surreal.

"No, thanks, I'm okay. I...ah..." I proffer the flowers. "I bought you these."

Vivian gives them a dismissive glance, then fixes her gaze directly on me.

"To what do I owe the pleasure?" She begins lighting a cigarette.

"Well, I kind of wanted to talk to you about something." I sit back down, placing the flowers beside me, I take a deep breath, then look Vivian directly in the eye.

"I talked to Uncle Ben, and he told me about what happened when James was small."

"What happened when James was small?" She flicks ashes.

I look at her, bewildered for an instant, and decide to take a different tack.

"I just wanted to let you know that I really care about your son. I know you know I love him; I mean you were at the wedding and all..."

Vivian sniffs.

"...But I want you to know how much I care about him, and that I would do anything to make him happy."

Vivian takes a long pull on her drink and begins to look uncomfortable.

"You probably figured that out on the first night of Hanukkah." I attempt a laugh and a conspiratory smile, but it's a no-go with Vivian. Vivian levels her gaze on me.

"I don't think you know my son the way I do." She punctuates her sentence by the putting down of her glass.

I'm not sure what to say and it takes a few seconds to respond. I nod my head and then lean directly over the coffee table, forcing Vivian to look in my eyes.

"And I don't think you know James the way I do. You're not supposed to. You're his mother; I'm his wife. In case you're not aware these are two different entities." I rise up from the couch, Vivian still staring at me, her mouth agape, her expression slightly stunned.

I continue.

"What I do know about James is that he doesn't like this displaced animosity towards me. You have a choice, Vivian. You can continue to act as if I am the enemy, and perhaps you'll win something, but I assure you it will be a hollow victory on your end. Or you can choose to embrace me, knowing that I have your son's best interests at heart, and be a part of the life we've begun together." I step away from the couch and begin gathering up my coat and purse. I take the flowers and thrust them towards Vivian, who is no longer looking in my direction. "I bought these for you. I hope you enjoy them."

With this, I exit the house and make my way down the path to my car. I'm trembling, but I feel good. Lighter. Better.

Chapter Twenty-Nine

It's the last night of Hanukkah and I'm settled on the couch in a pair of comfy sweats, my hair pulled back in a ponytail, fuzzy slippers on my feet. James is settled next to me with a ball cap on, quietly watching a bowl game on TV.

My phone rings and I lean over James to grab it.

"Hello, sister! Are you coming?"

"Yes, we're coming. Do you seriously not want me to bring anything? And what are you wearing?"

I looks down at my very comfy outfit.

"I think I'm wearing sweats."

"Oh, please." Dez doesn't believe me.

"I am. I just want this to be...the Anti-Hanukkah."

"Well, let's not say that in mixed company. It sounds vaguely Anti-Semetic."

I laugh, then reiterate.

"I mean it, Dez. Just bring yourself. Come as you are. I'll see you at seven."

"We'll be there."

I put down the phone and smile languidly over to James.

"What time did you tell Uncle Ben and Aunt Bunny?"

"Seven."

"Great, and your Mom and Vlad?"

"I don't know if they'll show."

"That's fine too. I've ordered enough pizza for everyone. Hey, you okay with this?" I turn James' face away from the game and force him to look directly at me.

"I am so fine. I think..." he says as he hops off the couch, grabs the remote, and then walks into the kitchen to grab a beer, "...all holidays should be like this."

I smile to myself and hug the throw pillow.

Soon we're hanging out on the couch, chatting with Dez and Jack. My Dad is in the adjacent dining room, putting a slice of pizza on a paper plate. He's making casual conversation with Uncle Ben and Aunt Bunny. In the background, we hear Adam Sandler's "The Hanukkah Song." Everyone is dressed down and there is a relaxed mood in the air. Grandma is sitting at the head of the table, wolfing down a slice of pepperoni and slugging back a beer.

"Miss Golden, this is my kind of holiday. Say, do you guys do this every year for Hanukkah?" Dad says this with a genuine smile.

"I wish!" Uncle Ben has a twinkle in his eye as he turns to Dad and says, "See what you've been missing out on?"

They all chuckle, as I lift myself off the couch and reach for a fistful of chips on a nearby table. I look at the clock, then turn to James.

"When do you want to light the candles?"

"We can do it now, if you'd like."

Just then the doorbell rings, and James and I share a look. As James goes to answer it, I lock eyes with Dez.

I shrug.

A moment later, Vivian and Vlad enter, and everyone takes a minute to greet them. Vivian looks at me purposefully, then nods her head, her eyes saying more than words.

I nod in return.

Soon, we all make our way into the dining room, where the Menorah is displayed in the center of the table.

"Uncle Ben, would you like to say the prayers in Hebrew?" James suggests.

"I would like to; I simply don't remember. How about some trusty old English?"

"That'll work."

Everyone gathers around the table as James lights from the shamash, one candle and then the next, until all nine candles are lit.

"Blessed are You, Lord, Our God, King of the Universe, who performed miracles for our ancestors in those days at this time," Uncle Ben intones.

Everyone says, "AMEN!"

A moment later I take a look around the room, and as I take it all in, I find myself touched beyond measure. I see James, illuminated by the glow of the candles, and I lean into him and whisper,

"This is perfect."

The End

Acknowledgements

"In all thy ways acknowledge Him, and He shall direct thy paths." (Proverbs 3:6)

With gratitude to the people who encouraged me to take action, those who cheered me on, and the reader…for letting me tell you a story.

Elizabeth Browning was instrumental in planting this very valuable seed: *"Anything is Possible, and Everything is Okay."*

Lindsay Miserandino: Yes…there's a story. AND I SHALL TELL IT IN ALL CAPS. Once again, you're amazing. Thanks for getting my particular brand of humor.

There are uncles…and then there's Uncle Benny. Simply the best. Hope you liked your namesake.

To THE CLASS: You all rock. You are tremendous artists and I am humbled to be in your presence.

And to all the Merry Hanukkah couples; I am forever blessed to know you. Keep holding it down. Remember God loves you. Period.

Made in United States
North Haven, CT
21 November 2022

27033910R00081